"Come on we need t downstairs dragging my "I'm coming keep you cousin Roxy waits pa~~tiently~~ downstairs holding a box "the delivery men have left already so let's go or they will get there before us" I roll my eyes and take a deep breath before looking around the house I had been living in the last 4 weeks "I'm ready" I walk towards the door and she follows closing and locking the door behind her. I walk down the stairs and open the boot of the car and stick my suitcase in before walking towards the passenger side and sitting down "so how far away are we going this time?" Roxy gets into the car and smiles "the furthest away so far" she sticks her belt on and smiles "hopefully this is the last time we will have to move." I lean back and look towards the empty house and smile softly "and maybe this time I can actually make friends and stay long enough to start school" Roxy's starts the car and drives down the street "I hope so too kiddo." We get onto the motorway and Roxy hands me an envelope "what's this?" I take it and open it "new identity" I look at the passport and documents "what? Why?" She takes a deep breath and shrugs "changing our second name clearly hasn't stopped Nathan from finding us" I look at the passport and nod "Amy Thomas? Sounds perfect" I rub her arm and stick the passport back "so what's yours?" She holds up another passport and smirks "I am now Roxy Thomas" I raise my eyebrow and smirk "Roxy?" She rolls her eyes and scoffs "I wanted something cool and I always liked that name" I smile and stick the documents back in the envelope and in the glove box "so where are we going this time?" Roxy smiles and hands me a piece of paper with a house on the front of its "Montana" I look at her and raise my eyebrows "that's like 12 hours away?" She smiles and reaches into the back seat and hands me a blanket "good job I came prepared" she grabs a bag of snacks and shakes her head "we need to get away far enough that they won't find us" I grab the bag and get a chocolate bar out and smile "your right. It will be good" I lean back and eat my chocolate bar "going further away will stop him finding me" I smile and shake my head "us." She smiles softly and I lean my head on the window "I don't think I could do this without you" she shrugs and smirks "what are little cousins for ehh?" I lean over and hug her and she continues to drive down the highway. After a few hours she pulls of the highway and I see a sign for Casper "why are we stopping?" She nods towards the bag and shakes her head "we need proper food in us" I smile and stick the bag down "yeah I am hungry" she nods towards her phone and smiles "text the delivery driver and text him that we are stopping but if he wants to keep going we will catch up" I grab her phone and shake my head "catch up? They will be miles ahead of us" Roxy looks out the window and shakes her head "no we passed them a few hours ago so they are pretty far behind" I smile and hand her the phone "done." She pulls into a small town and stops at the side of the sidewalk rolling her window down "excuse me?" A man walks over and smiles "hello ladies how can I help youse?" Roxy smiles and looks around "where's good to eat around here?" The man smiles and points down the road "Sherries Place. It's just down the road and turn right on Yellowstone highway" Roxy smiles and waves "thank you" she rolls the window back up and drives down the street looking around "Yellowstone Highway" she nods towards a sign and drives down it "there" I spot a little cafe with the sign Sherries Place and smile "looks nice" Roxy parks the car and smiles "let's go" she gets out the car and I follow her towards the door. A woman approaches us and smiles "table for 2?" Roxy smiles and nods "yes please" the waitress leads us to a table at the side of the restaurant and hands us menus "can I get youse a drink while youse wait?" I smile and look at the menu "can I have a can of cola please" Roxy smiles and nods "make that 2" the waitress walks away and I look at the menu "so I have good news" I look at Roxy and smile "what"? She smirks and sticks her menu down "you start school Monday" I smirk and shake my head "really?!" The whole restaurant looks at us and I stick my head down and smile "yeah" she takes a deep breath and lifts her menu up again "I have a good feeling about this time" I stick my menu up and smile "I hope your right" I shake my head and smile "wait doesn't school finish for the summer in two weeks?" Roxy nods and smiles "yeah so you have a two-week trail thing before summer then you start properly after then I guess" I smile and nod "can't wait." After we finish our food and Roxy stands up and hands me her purse "I'm going to the rest room but this ones on me ok kiddo?" I roll my eyes and smile "yes but stop calling me kiddo" I smirk and lean back "I'm 16 now so you can't call me that" she smirks and walks towards the bathroom "ok kiddo" she walks into the bathroom door and I roll my eyes and lean forward. The waitress walks over and smiles "was everything ok?" She takes the plates and I smile "yeah thank you. can we get the bill please" she smiles and hands me a piece of paper and walks away with the plates, I look at the bill and take a $20 from Roxy's purse and place it on top of the bill and the waitress walks back and takes it "keep the change" she smirks and nods "thank you" she walks away and I stick my jacket back on as Roxy walks back out from the bathroom "ready?" I smile and stand up "yeah" she grabs her jacket and purse and walks towards the door and I follow behind her. We get back into the car and she checks her phone "delivery driver texted me 10 minutes ago saying he just passed Jasper so we will catch up on him" I smile and stick my seatbelt on "ok" I look at the piece of paper with the house on it again and smile "so what's my room like?" Roxy smiles and shrugs "I've only seen pictures but the rooms are pretty big and the one room has an ensuite so we can argue about who gets that" I smile and nod "tags!" She rolls her eyes and sighs "fine but I want the large closet" I raise my eyebrow and smile "what large closet?" She starts the car and smiles "you will see" she drives towards the highway and I lean back and lean my head against the window "wake me up when we get there" I close my eyes and drift off to sleep. Roxy wakes me up and smiles softly "we are here" I open my eyes and look around "already?" She smiles and shakes her head "you have been sleeping for the last 6 hours" she nods towards the boot "I unpacked a few things and just waiting for the removal man now" she looks down the street and smiles "and here he is" I look down the street and see the removal man coming down with his van "ok well I will come help now" I get out the car and stretch before looking towards the house "looks nice and big compared to the last ones." Roxy comes and joins me on the sidewalk and looks at the house "it is" she points towards the back yard and smiles "it has a large back yard too so could get that dog you wanted" I roll my eyes and scoff "yeah until we move again and we need to leave it behind" the van stops and Roxy smiles and shakes her head "we won't have to move again" she walks towards the van and smiles softly "I promise this time will be different and no one will find us." I walk towards the van and lift up a box "where will I stick this?" Roxy picks up a box and nods towards the house "follow me" I smile and follow her towards the house and into the front door "stick everything in this room and we can sort it out later" I stick the box down and walk back out towards the van as the two men push in hand trolleys with five boxes each "where will we stick these?" Roxy comes out the living room and smiles "in here" they walk past me and walk into the living room and I walk back out towards the van and grab another box. "That looks heavy" I jump and turn around and see a beautiful boy with these big bright green eyes standing behind me at the side of the sidewalk. After looking at him for a few seconds I shake my head and scoff "what?" he nods towards the box and smiles "you want some help?" I look at the box and shake my head "no I'm ok thank you" I walk towards the house and place the box down "where will I stick this?" I turn around and see the boy standing by the door "what?" Roxy comes out from the kitchen holding cans of lemonade "who's this?" She smiles at me and I shake my head "I don't know" the boy walks into the living room and places the box down before shaking his hands "hello Miss I'm Brody James" he walks towards her and holds his hand out "James?" He smiles and she nods "you are our neighbour?" Brody smiles "yes Miss me and my older brother live next door" Roxy smiles and shakes her head "please call me Roxy" he looks at me and smirks "and you are?" I scoff and shake my head "going to bring more box's in" I walk out and walk towards the van and pick up another box "wow" I pick up a heavy box and nearly drop it "I got it" I feel hands under my hands and someone grab the box weight "thanks" I see Brody standing at the other side of the box "your welcome" he smirks and I roll my eyes and grab a lighter box "I'm Amy" I walk into the house with the box and stick it on the floor next to the other. The delivery men come back in and smile "we can get the rest if youse want to start unpacking?" Roxy looks at me and I shrug "yeah may as well start" Roxy nods and smiles "thank you" the men smile and walk back outside and I grab a box and look at it "bedroom 1" I look at Roxy and smile "that your bedroom I take it?" She smiles and takes the box "yeah that's fine" she walks up the stairs and I grab another box with bedroom 2 on it and smile "now I can go see my new bedroom" I walk upstairs and see Roxy in one of the rooms "so what one is my room?" She walks out her bedroom and smiles "the last room on the right" I look down the hallway and smile "thank you." I walk down the hallway and open the last door on the right and see a large room with freshly painted grey walls "this is perfect!" I smile and walk in and stick the box at the back of the room and see two doors at the side of the room "I'm guessing one of these lead into the bathroom" I open the first door and see a cupboard with shelves already build in "this room just gets better and better" I close the first cupboard and open the second door and see a bathtub and a toilet and sink "yip I love it here" I close the door and walk down the hallway towards Roxy "I love it here" she smiles and nods "I knew you would" I walk into her freshly painted purple room and look around "I have grey walls" she smiles and looks around "I didn't choose it" I shrug and smirk "I like it though" she smiles softly and nods "good" she nods towards the door and shrugs "shall we finish unpacking?" I smile and nod "yeah" I walk downstairs and she follows behind me and I grab another box "will we start with down here first?" I look at the box's and nod "ok" I grab a box with kitchen on it and walk towards the door "I will do the kitchen and you do the living room?" She grabs a box which says living room and nods "ok." I walk into the kitchen and look around the open space "nice" I smile and stick the box on the counter and open it and see glass tumblers so I look around the cupboard and smile "does it matter where things go?" I look at the cupboard at the end and walk towards it and open it "no just stick them anywhere!" I nod and grab the glasses and stick them in the cupboard before heading back into the living room and grabbing another box "where did your friend go too?" I look around and shrug "he's not my friend but I don't know" I walk back towards the kitchen and open the box again and see plates so stick them in the cupboard next to the glass tumblers and walk back into the living room and grab another box and unpack it. I walk back into the living room and the removal men carry in the sofa "where is this going?" Roxy looks around and nods towards the back of the living room "just leave it there and I'll sort it out" the men stick the sofa down and I smile "that's all the box's done so we just have the furniture now" Roxy nods and smiles "thank you" she unpacks another box and I grab another marked kitchen and walk into it and place it onto the kitchen unit before starting to unpack it. Roxy walks in and hands me a blind for the window "you able to stick this on?" I look at the window and nod "yeah" she smiles and walks back out and I look at it and shake my head and walk towards the window and climb on the counter and stick the blind up and walk back into the living room and see Roxy separating the box's "done the kitchen blinds" she smiles and hands me a box "there is no more kitchen box's so you can move onto your room" she nods towards the front door and smiles "the removal men have already stuck your bed upstairs in your room so It's just your drawers and whatever other furniture you have to come" I nod and smile "ok well I will go start unpacking my room" she grabs a box and nods towards the door "I'm going to do mine too so after you." I walk upstairs and head into my room and stick the box on my bed and open it and see photo frames and smile when I see a picture of me and my parents when I was younger "do you want too" Roxy walks in holding a set of curtains smiling "that was the day your dad took you too the shooting range for the first time" I smile and stick it back in the box "my dad loved that place" she walks over and sits down next to me "I know you secretly loved it too" I laugh softly and nod "I loved it more knowing my dad loved it" I stand up and the removal men walk in with a set of drawers "where is this going?" Roxy stands up and smiles "my room" she hands me the curtains and nods towards my window "you want to stick them up? I'm not too keen on the height" I roll my eyes and smile "yeah I'll do them all" she smiles and walks out the room and down the hall. I grab the curtains and stick them through the curtain pole before walking towards the window and standing on top of the ledge and stick the curtains up, I look out the window and see Brody in the window across from me with his shirt of and I freeze and smirk. I shake my head and take a deep breath "no boys" I nod firmly and look back towards the curtain and stick them up, I look back at the window and see him doing pull ups on a bar in his room "oh come on!" He looks at me and I smirk and shake my head and try get down but fall flat on my face "ouch" Roxy runs in and looks around "what was that?" I stand up and laugh nervously "I fell" she tries to hold her laugh in and shakes her head "are you ok?" I nod and smile "yeah I'm fine" I brush myself down and she nods and walks back out the room "are you ok?!" I roll my eyes before turning around towards the window and see Brody with his window opened leaning out his "god could this get any worse" I open my window opening it "yes I'm fine thank you" I close the window and close the curtains before turning around and rubbing my arm "ouch" I take a deep breath and head back downstairs and grab another box but drop it at the bottom of the stairs "wow" Brody catches it and smiles "I got it" he looks at my arm and nods "you sure you're ok? My brothers a doctor so he can have a look at your arm if you want?" I smile and shake my head taking the box "I'm sure I'm fine" he shrugs and walks towards the living room and grabs a box "well I'm free all afternoon so I don't mind helping you with these and whatever else youse need" I roll my eyes and see Roxy coming down stairs "hey Brody" he looks at her and smiles "hey Roxy" he lifts the box up and shrugs "Amy hurt her arm when she fell look at" he looks at me and smirks "something" he looks at Roxy again and shrugs "so I offered my help if that's ok?" Roxy raises her eyebrow and looks at me "and Amy agreed to let you help?" I roll my eyes and walk upstairs "no I didn't but he's not taking no for an answer so he can help you and stay out my way" I walk towards my room and stick the box on my bed and sit next to it taking a deep breath rubbing my arm. "Is she always like that?" Roxy grabs a box and walks up the stairs with Brody behind her "what? stubborn? yes" Brody follows Roxy into her room and sticks the box down "I was going to say independent but yeah that too" Roxy smiles and nods "yeah she's always been like that" she walks back out the room and down the stairs "but other than that she's pretty cool" I walk towards my door and hear her "please don't tell me she's playing cupid with the next door neighbour?" I take a deep breath and walk out the room and smile towards them before heading downstairs and grabbing another box. The removal men walk back in with my drawers and looks at Roxy "where do these go?" Roxy points towards my room "the back room" the men walk up and I smile and grab another box "time to make my room feel a bit like home" I smirk towards Brody and nod "for now" I walk upstairs and into my room as the removal men walk out. Brody looks at Roxy and shrugs "for now? Do's youse travel a lot then?" Roxy coughs and laughs nervously "yeah we have done the last 2 years" she shakes her head and grabs another box "but I plan on sticking around here for a while" Brody grabs a box and follows Roxy upstairs and looks towards my room smiling "good." I take a duct tape of my drawers and place my photo frames around my room and place the photo of me and my parents on my bedside drawer before taking a deep breath and heading downstairs "Roxy?" I walk into the Living room and see Roxy unconscious on the sofa "Roxy?!" I run over towards her and shake her "where will I stick these?" I turn around and see Brody with a pile of towels "what happened?" He looks over and smiles "take it she took my advice" I stand up and shake my head "what?" He places the towels on the table and nods towards Roxy "she said she was feeling tired so I told her to take a rest and have a nap after the removal men left" I shake my head and look at Roxy "that doesn't sound like Roxy" Brody walks towards me and shakes his head "what?" I look at him and shake my head "get out" he scoffs and smiles "what?" I shove him and shake my head "get out!" He holds his hands up and nods "ok" he walks towards the door but turns around and smiles "I'm sorry" I walk towards the door and shake my head "whatever" I slam the door and run upstairs and into my room. After a few hours I finally finish unpacking the last box and everything looks more like a home and not a garage sale, I walk into the kitchen and check the cupboards and realise they are empty "pizza it is" I walk into the living room and sit on the other sofa and grab my phone and check for a local pizza place and ring them "hello your through too Alexandra's can I take your order please" I look at Roxy and smile "can I have a large pepperoni pizza" I look around and see my bag in the corner of the room "what's the address?" I laugh nervously and shake my head looking around "I'm not sure" the man on the other line takes a deep breath and scoffs "stop wasting our time please" they hang up and I shake my head "guess I'm collecting." I grab Roxy's phone and stick it next to her and grab my phone and text her "going for food in case you wake up and worry. Won't be long x" I smile and walk out the door and head down the street. I walk into a small town and see a pizza place "that will do" I walk into it and see Brody speaking to the man behind the counter and I catch the man's attention "hello miss what can I get you?" I smile and walk over towards the counter "can I have a large pepperoni pizza" the man raises his eyebrow and smiles "did you call in about 10 minutes ago?" I smirk and nod "yeah I just moved here that's why I didn't know my address" he smirks and nods "my apologies for being so rude" I smile and shake my head "no It's my apologies for calling without realising." The man sticks my order in and smiles "$8 please" I hand him $10 and smile "keep the change." Brody looks at me and smiles "you want a ride home?" He nods towards the motorbike outside "no I'm good" I shake my head and look towards the screen with my order on it "do you know the way back?" I scoff and smile "yes" he nods slowly and smiles "ok" a man comes over with 2 boxes of large pizzas and hands them too Brody "your loss" he leaves and gets on his motorbike and drives of. "Your friends with Brody?" I look at the man behind the counter and shake my head "no he's my neighbour" he smiles and writes something down "now I know your address can I get a name?" I smile and nod "Amy Thomas" he writes it down and smirks "I'm Joseph Petro" I smile and nod "nice to meet you" the same man who brought Brody's pizzas out comes out holding a large pizza box "here you go Miss" I smile and take the box "thank you" the man behind the counter and waves "bye Amy" I smile and wave "bye Joseph" I walk out the door closing it behind me and walk back down the direction I came from. I get to the bottom of my street and smile "getting used to these directions" I smirk and stroll along the street "who needs Brody" I jump when I hear a loud bang from behind me and turn around and see a shadow a few meters behind me, I walk faster but the shadow walks faster too and I hear footsteps right behind me so I hide behind a bin and jump out from behind the bin and punch hitting something "ouch!" They fall to the ground and I stand up properly and look towards them and see Brody lying on the ground with blood running down his nose. "What the hell Brody?" I hold my hand out and he takes it and rubs his face "why are you following me?" He shakes his head and smirks "too make sure you got home ok" I shake my head and pick up my pizza "I told you I would" he smiles softly and shrugs "I know. I'm sorry" I roll my eyes and walk down the street "well just stay away from me" he takes a deep breath before rubbing his nose again "ok I get the message" I open my gate and walk towards the door looking towards him "get some ice on that" he nods and rubs his nose "I will don't worry" I smirk and look down "sorry" he smiles softly and stops at his front door "It's fine" he shrugs and takes a deep breath "I'm fine" I open my door and nod "goodnight" he smiles and waves "goodnight." I walk in and see Roxy wasn't on the sofa anymore "hello? I'm back" she runs downstairs smiling "about time" she walks into the kitchen and grabs two glasses and a bottle of cola "I got bored so made the beds and stuff" I sit down and shake my head "how long was I away for?" She sits down and smirks "not long but I woke up right after you left" she pours me a drink and hands me it "what happened?" She shakes her head and grabs my hand "oh I kind of punched Brody" she shakes her head and raises her eyebrows "what? why?" I roll my eyes and sit the pizza on my knee and open it "he was in the pizza place and offered me a ride home but I said no so he must have drove home on his motorbike and ran back to check on me" I shrug and take a deep breath "I thought he was a thug so I hid behind a bin and attacked him when he came close enough" Roxy smirks and nods eating into a slice of pizza "that's my girl!" I look at my hand and shake my head "his nose looked pretty bad but I'm sure he will live" I eat a slice of pizza and look at the front door and smile. "Goodnight Roxy!" I walk into my room and close my bedroom door slightly and walk towards my drawers getting a large top and getting changed, I take my top of and look out the window and see Brody doing more pull ups "is that all he does?" I smirk and stare at him "probably working of that pizza" I look down towards my flat stomach and squeeze out "I will go for a jog" I look towards the chocolates Roxy left on my bed and smirk "soon" I sit on the edge of the bed and take my trousers of and stand up and see Brody at his window smiling towards me "hey!" I quickly sit back down and stick the large t-shirt on my covering my pants and walk towards the window and open it "I saw you watching me don't worry" he winks and leans out his window "you wish" I smirk and close my window and curtains and turn around "no boys" I smirk and shake my head "definitely no boys" I take a deep breath and walk towards the bathroom and brush my teeth before turning my light out and getting into bed drifting of straight away.

I wake up the next morning when I hear loud music coming from outside "who is playing music so loud at this time?" I stand up and walk towards the window and see Brody's window wide open and music coming from his room "hey!" He pops his head up topless and smirks "afternoon" I shake my head and lean out the window "what are you talking about? Turn that music down" he smirks and nods towards his watch "It's 1:30PM and I need to get my work out done" I roll my eyes and close my window "jerk" I look towards my alarm clock and shake my head "did I really sleep till 1:30?" I take a deep breath and grab clothes and get changed before running downstairs. I look in the living room and shake my head "hello?" Roxy pops out from the kitchen and waves "in here" I walk in and see Roxy sitting at the table writing a list "what you doing?" She smiles and shrugs "doing a shopping list" I look towards the fridge and open it "yeah we really do need food" I walk towards her and look at the list "oh can you see if they have any of the little mint chocolate things I liked when we were in Texas?" Roxy laughs sarcastically and shakes her head "you are coming with me" I nod and smile "fine let me just get my coat and shoes" I run upstairs and grab my jacket from the back of my door and grab my shoes from the bottom of the window and see Brody in his room on the phone look stressed pacing his room "wonder what's wrong with him" I shake my head and stick my shoes on before heading out my bedroom door and downstairs. I look into the kitchen and smile "ready?" Roxy walks out the kitchen sticking the piece of paper in her bag and smiling "yeah let's go" I open the door and walk towards her car and see Brody run out his house with a concerned look slamming the door behind him and getting onto his motorbike "hey Brody" Roxy looks at him and waves smiling "hey girls" he smiles and sticks his helmet on before driving of "what's his problem?" I shrug and open the car door "I don't know" I get into the car and she starts it and drives down the street "do you know where you are going?" She smirks and shakes her head "nope" she smiles and takes a deep breath "but I'm sure we will find something" I look around and smile "yeah probably miles away" she nods towards down the street and smirks "found one" I look over and smile and see a supermarket "or not." She parks into the car park and grabs her bag "let's go" I get out the car and follow her into the supermarket and grab a trolley "so what's first on the list?" After a long walk around the supermarket we finally finish and drive home "I'm glad I found they chocolate mints" Roxy smirks and nods "me too" she laughs sarcastically and sticks the bags on the kitchen counter "It's all you went on about" I stick the bags on the other counter and shrug "well they are amazing" we start unpacking when the doorbell rings "I will get it" I run towards the door and open it and see Brody "hey" he smiles softly and takes a deep breath "can I come in?" I look into the kitchen towards Roxy and she nods "yeah" I open the door wide and let him in "my older brother wanted to invite youse over for dinner tonight if youse fancy it? He makes the best mac and cheese" Roxy looks at me and shrugs "I love mac and cheese so we would love to" Brody looks at me and smiles "sure have nothing else planned" he nods and waves "ok well have a nice day girls" he walks out the door and I close it behind him and shake my head and walk into the kitchen "is it just him and his brother?" Roxy shrugs and smiles softly "I don't know" she looks out the kitchen window and smiles "but I hope his brother is as hot as him but a lot older" I roll my eyes and open another bag and finish unpack the rest of the shopping. We finish sticking the shopping away and I grab a bottle of water and head towards the stairs "I'm going for a quick bath and then we can go over to Brody's." Roxy smiles and walks towards me "ok" she shrugs and laughs nervously "should we take something over with us?" I nod towards the kitchen and smirk "you still got that bottle of wine you got in Texas that you didn't like but bought because the guy who tried to sell you it was hot?" Roxy looks towards the kitchen and smirks "yeah and he was really hot wasn't he?" I roll my eyes and walk upstairs "boys are trouble" she leans up the stairs and smiles "doesn't stop you being attracted to them." I head into my bedroom slightly closing the door behind me and walk into the bathroom leaving the door open and run a bath, I walk back into the bedroom and look through my clothes and shake my head "Roxy?" I walk out the door and shake my head "can I borrow something to wear? I left all my nice clothes behind" she smiles and nods "yeah" she walks down the hallway and opens a closet door and I walk in and see a large walk in wardrobe "wow" she smirks and nods "I know!" She walks in and looks around "this is the large closet I was telling you about" I look around and smile "could turn this into a guest bedroom" Roxy walks in and grabs a black skin-tight dress "yeah with all the guest's we have coming to stay" I take the dress and smile "true" I look at the dress and take a deep breath "trust you too pick this dress" she rolls her eyes and turns me around shoving me out "just get changed" I smile and shake my head "I'm going I'm going" I walk towards my bedroom and stick the dress on my bed before heading into the bathroom stopping the bath and closing the door slightly. After Roxy tries on a lot of outfits we finally get ready to leave "let's go let's go!" I run downstairs and grab my shoes "you are not wearing them" I look at my shoes and shake my head "It's all I brought with me" she rolls her eyes and heads into the kitchen "I knew you would say that so I got you these" she hands me a bag and I open it and see a pair of black heels "thank you" I hug her and sit down and stick them on "now are we ready?" She smiles and nods "yes" she grabs her lipstick and sticks it in her bag and walks towards the door "oh grab the wine" I walk back into the kitchen and look around "where is it?" She opens the front door and looks back "by the window" I look over towards the window and see the bottle of wine so I grab it and look out the back window and see Brody outside the back pacing up and down on the phone "you get it?" I smile and nod "yeah" I run out the kitchen and follow her out the door before closing and locking the door behind me. Roxy walks out the gate and I smile and climb the fence and smile "hurry up" she looks at me and shakes her head "your so like your father" I pull my dress down and smirk "well thank you" she joins me at the front door and shrugs "never said that was a compliment" I shove her and knock the door. Brody opens the door and smiles "hey ladies" he opens the door and wide and smiles at me before shaking his head "please come in" he stands behind the door still looking at me and closes it behind us "my brother is just finishing up so if youse would like to sit at the table and I can get youse a drink?" Roxy smiles and nods "ok" she looks at me and raises her eyebrows "the wine?" I shake my head and smile "oh yeah" I hand Brody the bottle and wine and smile "here" he smirks and takes the bottle touching my hand for a few seconds before pulling away "thank you." He points down the hallway and smiles "this way ladies" we follow him down the hallway and he points towards a room and opens the door "just wait in here and I will get youse a drink? what would youse like?" Roxy smiles and nods "beer" I roll my eyes and smile " just a cola for me" she nods slowly and smiles before walking into the room at the end of the hallway. I look at the room door and smile "let's get this over with" Roxy laughs nervously and walks in "play nice" I walk in and smile "always" I sit down across from Roxy and look around "I think the brother might have a girlfriend" Roxy shakes her head and looks around "what makes you think that?" I shrug and smile towards her "place feels like there's a women's touch about it" she rolls her eyes and leans back "that's ridiculous" I lean forward and shrug "we will soon see then" she looks towards the door and smirks "might be Brody who has a girlfriend" I lean back and shrug "I wouldn't care" she smirks and nods slowly "you aren't fooling me." The door opens and Brody walks in holding a can of beer and cola "here youse go ladies" he hands us them and I smile "thank you" he sits next to me and smiles "Jeremy is just coming" I smile and nod "will it just be Jeremy joining us?" Brody nods "yes why?" I lean back and shrug "not his girlfriend?" I look at Roxy and smirk "no" Brody laughs nervously and shakes his head "he doesn't have a girlfriend" Roxy smirks and leans forward "will your girlfriend not be joining us?" The door opens and a man who looks just older than Brody walks in holding a tray of plates laughing sarcastically "Brody having a girlfriend?" Roxy looks at me and smiles "so It's just the two of youse?" He looks at me and sticks the tray down "yeah just the two of us" he sits down next too Roxy and nods "yeah" he hands the plates out and smiles "hope youse like it" I look at the plate of mac and cheese and smile "It's my favourite" I grab a fork and eat a bite. After we all finish Jeremy takes the plates and smiles "I will just get rid of these" he looks at Brody and nods "you want to go into the living room and sit? I will bring that lovely looking wine you brought in?" Roxy looks at me and smiles "Roxy is on a non-wine diet" she looks at Jeremy and nods "yeah" she holds her beer up and shrugs "another beer will be fine" Jeremy looks at me and smiles "another cola?" I smile and nod "yes please" he walks out the room and Brody stands up "shall we?" Roxy stands up and walks out the room and Brody smiles and looks at me "a non-wine diet?" I smirk and look down "I know she's a little weird" I laugh nervously and follow him out the room and towards the living room. I sit down on the sofa next too Roxy and Jeremy walks in holding two cans of beer and two cans of cola and hands me and Roxy a can "thank you" he sits down on the single chair and leans back "so is it just youse two?" Roxy leans back and smiles "yeah" he looks at me and smirks "and are youse sisters?" Roxy shakes her head "no cousins" she looks at me and smiles softly "but like sisters" I smile softly and nod "what about youse?" Jeremy leans forward and opens the beer "just the two of us" he looks at Brody and nods slowly "our parents both died 6 years ago and It's been us ever since" Roxy leans forward and smile softly "aww I'm sorry to hear that" he smiles softly and nods "thank you. We have two cousins who lives in foster care but we hardly see them" I look at Brody and he smiles softly at me "so what made you come too Montana?" Roxy shrugs and leans back "just caught my eye and I wanted something different." She looks at Brody and smiles "what age are you Brody?" I nearly choke on my cola and shake my head "16" she looks at me and smiles "same age as Amy" she looks back at Brody "so you still go to school?" He looks at me and nods "yes" he looks back at Roxy and she smiles "Amy is starting school Monday so maybe you could show her around?" He looks at me and smirks "I would love too" I look at Roxy and roll my eyes "perfect" she smirks and drinks her beer. I look at Brody and smile "can I use your bathroom?" Jeremy stands up and smiles

"I will show you where it is" I smile and stand up "thank you" he leads towards the stairs and I follow him up then "just in there" he points down the hallway and smiles "second door on the right" I nod and smile "thank you" he walks back downstairs and I walk down the hallway and walk into the bathroom and close the door taking a deep breath "no boys no boys" I shake my head and walk towards the mirror and wash my face. Jeremy walks back downstairs and sits down "what happened to your parents?" Jeremy shakes his head and leans back "if you don't mind me asking?" Roxy shakes her head and smiles "no It's fine" she takes a long sip of her drink and nods "Amy's parents where both in a car accident two years ago and I never knew my parents. My mum is Amy's dad's sister so she left me with Amy's parents and they brought me up" Brody raises his eyebrows and leans back "that would explain why she's" I walk downstairs and shake my head "so what?" I scoff and they look at me "don't stop on my behalf" I look at Roxy and shake my head "I'm going home" I look at Jeremy and smile "thanks for dinner" I quickly walk towards the door and close it behind me. Brody stands up and runs towards the door "Amy wait!" He looks down the pathway and shakes his head "where did you go?" he looks over towards my house and sees me falling over the fence "Amy!" I stand up and shake my head "I'm fine" I take the heels of and walk towards the door and unlock it before slamming it behind me. Brody looks at the house and takes a deep breath "I'm sorry" he heads back inside and shakes his head "sorry if I upset her Roxy" he look over towards Roxy and sees her kissing Jeremy "really Jeremy?" Jeremy looks at him and shrugs "what?" Brody rolls his eyes and shrugs "just go work out or something dork" Brody rolls his eyes and walks towards the stairs "whatever" he runs upstairs and into his bedroom. He takes his top of and heads into the bathroom and runs the shower before closing the bathroom door. I get changed into some joggers and a jumper and sit on my bed and pick up my book and start reading it, after a few minutes I stick the book down and take a deep breath before looking around and standing up and heading out my bedroom

room and downstairs. I walk into the kitchen and grab my purse and keys and leave a note for Roxy "heading to the mall for new clothes for school. Won't be long x" I leave the note by the front door table and open the door and close it behind me. I walk down the street and walk towards the mall and reach for the door "It's closed!" I turn around and someone getting of a motorbike before taking their helmet of and I see a beautiful boy around my age "what?" He nods towards the mall door and smiles "the mall is closed" I look towards the door and see the opening times 8-6 "what time is it?" He looks at his watch and smiles "6:20" I smile and shake my head "thank you" I walk back towards the street and he drives towards me and stops beside me "I know another place that is open late if you need something?" He holds his helmet out and I smile and shake my head "what?" he shrugs and smiles "well you must need something important going to the mall at this time?" I look towards the mall and smile "just new clothes and stuff for starting school tomorrow" he smirks and pushes his helmet out more "school? I know the perfect place for a first day of school outfit and essentials" I take the helmet and shake my head "why not" I get on the back of his bike and he smiles "hold on" I cuddle into him and he starts the engine "don't be shy" I laugh nervously and shake my head "I'm fine" he nods and starts the engine "ok here we go then" he drives the motorbike down the street and I hold onto him tighter. After a few minutes he slows down and pulls into a car park by a small abended looking building "place looks empty and like It's been abended for years" I get of the bike and take the helmet of "it needs a little TLC but It's nice inside" I smile and nod "ok I will take your word for it" I hand him his helmet back and smile "well thanks for the ride but I'm sure I will be ok from here" he gets of the motorbike and sticks the helmet on the chair "I don't mind staying around and give you a ride back?" I raise my eyebrow and shrug "you don't have too" he smirks and nods "I know but I want too" I smile and take a deep breath "ok." I walk towards the mall and he follows "so did you just move too town?" I look at him and nod "yeah me and my cousin moved here yesterday" he opens the door and smiles "thank you" we walk in and I look down and laugh nervously "I didn't catch your name?" I look at him and he smiles "I'm" he looks in front of us and his face drops "Ryder!" I look over and see Brody walking towards us "what are you doing with her?" He looks at me and smirks "youse know each other?" I roll my eyes and look at Brody "he's my neighbour" he looks at me and nods "you live in the old" Brody shakes his head and coughs "go home Ryder" I look at Brody and shake my head "no" they both look at me and Ryder smiles "what?" I look at Brody and shake my head "no" I look at Ryder and smile "he's my ride" I laugh nervously "plus he's showing me around" Ryder looks at Brody and smirks "yeah what she said." Brody takes a deep breath and shakes his head "this isn't over" he walks out the door and I look at Ryder and smile "what was that about?" Ryder smirks and shrugs "his ex-left him for me and I don't think he got over it" I nod slowly and smile "you have a girlfriend?" He shakes his head and laughs nervously "no this was in middle school" I smile and nod "and he's still not over it?" Ryder shrugs and smirks "guess not." I smile and shake my head "let's go" I walk towards the shops and Ryder follows behind me "so I never got your name" I smirk and look down "Amy" he smiles softly and nods firmly "Amy. I like it" I scoff and shake my head "thanks" I look around and nod towards a girls clothes store "you don't have to come with me you know? I can't imagine this is how you want to spend your Sunday evening" he looks around and shakes his head "shopping? Oh yeah I love shopping" I smile and nod towards the girl's clothes shop "let's go then." I walk around the shop and pick up a few things and head towards the checkout desk "you not want to try them on?" I look at them and shake my head "no I'm good" he shrugs and smirks "ok your loss" I hand the clothes to the woman behind the counter and she smiles at Ryder and scans my stuff keeping looking at him "$43 please" I hand her the money and she smiles at me and gives me my change and bag before looking back towards Ryder "bye" she waves at him and he nods "bye" I smirk and shake my head walking out the store "that wasn't awkward at all" Ryder walks beside me and shakes his head "what?" I scoff and shake my head "she was clearly into you" he looks back towards the store and laughs nervously "what Katie? She was my mums' best friends' little girl so she is like a sister" I smile and shake my head "maybe you should tell her that" I look back and see her standing by the door smiling towards us, Ryder look over and laughs nervously "oh wow" he shakes his head and rushes of down the mall.

After dragging Ryder with me too a few stores I finally finish and we walk towards Ryders motorbike "how am I meant to carry then while holding onto you?" Ryder looks at my bags and smiles "I never thought of that" I laugh nervously and shake my head "It's fine I can call my cousin" he looks around and shakes his head "my friend Ricky is here I can give him a call and see if he can take you in his car?" I look around the car park and raise my eyebrows "my limit of getting into a stranger's vehicle a day is one sorry" he smirks and walks towards me taking my bags "I will come with you and I'll get him too drop me back of?" I take a deep breath and look around "ok" he smirks and nods "good" he gets his phone and smiles "won't be long" he walks towards a car a few spaces beside us and phones someone. I lean against the motorbike and look towards the door and see it open and a familiar face walk out 'what is he doing here? And who is she?' I stand up straight as I see Brody walk out the doors laughing with another girl 'why do I care? He can do what he wants' I scoff and lean back avoiding eye contact with him. "Amy?" I look up and see them walking towards me "why are you still here?" Brody walks over and smiles towards the girl "you want to wait by my motorbike?" The girl looks at me and smiles softly and innocently "yeah" she walks away and Brody looks around "you here alone?" I look towards Ryder and shake my head "no Ryder is just getting his friend too give me a lift" he looks towards Ryder and smiles "I can get Jeremy too come get you if you like?" I smile and shake my head "no that's ok" he shrugs and smiles softly "you sure?" I look back towards Ryder and see him shaking his head "yeah I'm sure Ryders friend will be here soon" he smiles softly and nods "ok" he shrugs and laughs softly "see you later then?" I smile softly and nod firmly "bye" he walks towards the direction the girl went and he gets on his motorbike and the girls gets on behind him and wraps her arms around his waist before they drive of. I look back towards the ground and take a deep breath 'maybe Roxy isn't a bad idea right now' I look at my phone and click on Roxy's name "here he is!" Ryder walks back over and looks towards the door and I see a boy walk out smiling towards us "Amy this is Ricky" the boy walks over smoking a fag before spitting it out and standing on it "nice to meet you" he holds his hand out and I smile and shake his hand "nice to meet you" he looks at Ryder and smirks "so this your new girl?" Ryder looks at me and smirks "nah she's too sweet and innocent" he grabs my bags and walks towards the car he was at before "let's go" I scoff and shake my head following him towards the car and get in the back. Ryder gets in the front and smiles at his friend "thanks for doing this man" he looks at me through the rear-view mirror "anytime" he smiles and nods firmly "so where we going?"

Ryder points down the car park and smiles "I will direct you" he looks at me and smirks "she will get you lost" I lean back and smirk. The whole way back Ryder and his friend talk about football "so are you going to bring your girl too the next game?" Ryder looks at me and smirks "she's not my girl" Ryder shrugs and leans back "I just met her" Ricky looks at me through the rear-view mirror and smirks "really?" I smile nervously and nod "well can she be my girl?" I roll my eyes and shake my head "no!" I look at Ryder and he looks at me smiling "she's a nice girl so I don't want her being played so she is of limits" I scoff and lean back smirking "I'm not a prize" Ryder looks me up and down and smiles "I know I didn't mean it like that" he looks at Ricky and smirks "I just don't want other boys thinking they have chance with you" I raises my eyebrows and look him up and down "and what makes you think you do?" He shrugs and smirks "why else would you get onto a stranger's motorbike if you didn't think there was something there" I shake my head and laugh nervously looks towards the ground "exactly" he turns around and smiles. "Isn't this where James stays?" we pull up outside and Ryder nods "she's his new neighbour" he looks at me and smiles "you moved into the old" Ryder shakes his head and Ricky looks at me and smiles "a lovely house" I raise my eyebrow and smirks "thank you" I grab my bags and get out and Ryder walks me too my gate "so I will see you tomorrow?" I smile and nod "I guess you will" he takes my hand and kisses it "until then" he smiles and walks back towards the car and I run into the house closing the door behind me. "And where have you been?" I turn around and see Roxy standing in the kitchen with her arms crossed "shopping" I hold my bags up and smile "oh" she shrugs and smile "ok" I run upstairs and stick my stuff away and grab my bag "can I come in?" Roxy pops her head in and I nod "yeah" she sits on my bed and I stick my new notebook and pens in my bag "get anything nice?" I shrug and look at my bags "just a few new clothes and school stuff" she smiles and looks at my bag "cute." She leans back and takes a deep breath "are you excited?" I shrug and sit down next to her "yeah" I laugh nervously and take a deep breath "I haven't been too school for the last 2 years so I'm a little nervous" she smiles and stokes my face "you will be fine" she stands up and shrugs "plus you know Brody" she walks towards the door and I smile and look down "and Ryder and Ricky" she raises her eyebrow and smiles "who?" I smile and look at her "met other people today when I was out shopping" she smirks and nods slowly "you still sticking by your motto?" I nod firmly and smile "no boys" she nods and smirks "new town means new rules" she leaves the room closing the door slightly behind her, I lie back on the bed and take a deep breath "not happening" I close my eyes and feel myself fall asleep before drifting of after a few seconds.

I wake up the next morning when I hear my room door open "time to get up for school" I stretch and sit up "I'm up" she walks back out the door and I stand up and grab clothes and get changed. I run downstairs with my bag and jacket and stick them at the bottom of the stairs "I've made you breakfast" I walk into the kitchen and see toast and peanut butter "thanks" I grab a slice of toast and nod "you dropping me of?" She smiles and nods "yeah. You ready?" I nod and walk out the door and she follow behind me and grabs her car keys "let's go then" I grab my bag and jacket and walk out the door closing it behind me and following Roxy towards her car and getting in it. Roxy drives of and I see Brody walk out his front door as we drive of "so are you excited?" I shrug and look at her "little nervous" she smiles and shrugs "you will be fine" I take a deep breath and smile "just hope I actually last here." We pull up outside the school and I smile "I will see you after school?" She smiles and nods "yeah" I get out the car and she shake her head "I have a job interview at 3 so you might need to make your own way home but I will text you and let you know ok?" I nod and smile "ok" I close the door behind me and walk towards the school entrance doors. I hear a motorbike drive into the car park and roll my eyes looking towards it as the rider gets of taking their helmet of and look towards me "hey Amy" Ryder walks towards me smiling "you want a personal tour?" I smile and nod my head "that would be great thanks" he opens the door and I walk through it and he points towards the reception desk "I take it you don't have a schedule or nothing yet?" I shake my head and smile "no" he nods towards the reception and I walk towards it and he follows. A boy who looks just older than us sits behind the desk and smiles as I approach "you must be Amy" I nod and smile "yeah that's me" he clicks a few buttons on the computer and prints of a sheet of paper "here you go" he hands me the sheets of papers and smiles "welcome too Flathead High school" I smile and nod "thank you" Rider rolls his eyes and the boy behind the desk smirks towards him "let's go" Rider wraps his arm around mine and we walk down the hallway.

"No point you trying to remember that because we stop for summer in two weeks so you will get a new one" I look at the schedule and smile "I know" I see Maths and English first and stick it in my pocket "I have a pretty good memory though" Rider smiles and nods towards the stairs "maths first?" I nod and walk with him "yeah" he walks up the stairs and walk down the corridor, I stop outside a door and nod towards it "this is me" he looks at the door and smirks "Mr Blackwood?" I nod and smile "yeah" he points towards the door across from my class and smirks "this is me" I look at the door and smile "Mrs Blackwood" he nods and smiles "husband and wife" I smile nervously and look down "I gathered that" he walks towards his classroom and waves "well I guess I will see you after class" I walk towards my class and smile softly "I guess you will." I open the door and see a man behind the desk writing down on a sheet of paper "I will be with you in a minute" not taking his eyes of the sheet of paper he holds his hand out and I smile nervously and walk towards the desk "yes?" He looks up and smiles "you must be Amy" I smile and nod "yeah that's me" he grabs a sheet of paper from his desk drawer and nods "just take a seat dear and the rest of the class with come soon" the bell rings and he nods "that will be them now" I smile and look around the class and sit at the back of the class "here you go" Mr Blackwood hands me a maths book and nods towards it "just fill in what you can and I can grade you on your work" I look at the book and nod "ok" he walks away and I open the book and grab a pen from my bag and start working on it. The rest of the class walks in and I stick my head up and see Ricky walking towards me smiling "hey you" he sits down next to me and I smile "hey" he looks at my book and shakes his head "Mr Blackwood got you doing freshman work" I look at the book and shrug "is this freshman work?" I sit back and shake my head "was wondering why it was easy" Ricky sits up and scoffs "I found it hard" I look back towards the book and fill the rest of it in "done!" I lean back and look up and see the full class looking at me "sorry" I laugh nervously and look towards my desk "I will take that" Mr Blackwood walks towards me and takes the book before walking back towards his desk and sits down "now what?" I look over towards Ricky and see him on his phone "nothing" he looks at me and I shake my head "what?" He smirks and nods "the last two weeks until summer we do nothing" I smile and lean back "in every class?" Ricky looks back towards his phone and shrugs "depends who your teacher is" he looks at me and shakes his head "did your old teacher never do this?" I laugh nervously and shake my head "I've been travelling recently so not been in a school in the last year" he raises his eyebrow and smiles "lucky for some" he turns back to his phone and I smile and lean forward and rest my head on my desk. I close my eyes and after a few minutes the bell rings and I jump and sit up "class over already?" Ricky stands up and smiles "yeah" he nods towards the door and smirks "you have a visitor" I stand up and look towards the door and see Ryder looking towards me smiling "bye" I smile at Ricky and wave "bye Ricky" I walk towards the door and Mr Blackwood walks towards me "Amy?" I turn around and smile "yeah?" He smirks and shakes his head "I got told you hadn't been in education in the last year?" I raise my eyebrows and smile "that's correct yes?" he holds the book up and smiles "this is amazing work" I laugh nervously and nod "with travelling and due to boredom I kept up with school work and done a lot of puzzles" he smiles and nods "well keep up the good work" I nod and smile "I will thank you" I turn around and walk towards Ryder smiling. "Hey" he smiles and I look at him and nod "hello" he nods towards the classroom and shrugs "so how was your first class?" I smirk and nod "not that bad actually" I walk towards the corridor and he follows "who you got for English?" I get my schedule from my jacket and look at its "Miss Duncan" he laughs softly and nods "same as me" I stick my schedule back into my pocket and look at him and smirk "lucky you." I follow him down the corridor and towards the English department and he stops and walks into a classroom and I bump into him as he walks in front of me "sorry" he shakes his head and smiles "It's ok" he nods towards the classroom "this is us" I walk into the classroom half packed but with no teacher "you can sit next to me" I smile and nod "ok" he walks towards a table by the window and pulls a chair out "here you go" I smile and sit down "thank you" I take my jacket of and he sits next to me and smiles. A girl walks over and sits on Ryders desk "hey Ryder!" Ryder rolls his eyes and leans back "hi Abbie" the girl flicks her long beautiful brown hair over her shoulder and flutters her eyelashes "you still on for studying at your place later?" She looks at me and smirks and I smile softly and look down "I can't I have plans" he looks at me and winks "really?" She looks me up and down and scoffs "maybe next time" she smirks at Ryder before walking towards the back of the class and sitting down. Ryder laughs nervously and looks down "that's my ex" I look at her and smile "the same ex that you and Brody used to date?" Ryder looks at her and nods "yeah that's her" she looks at us and flicks her long beautiful brown hair again before sitting down and joining in on the conversation with her friends. A young-looking woman rushes into the classroom carrying a large folder in one hand and holding her hair back from her face with the other "sorry I'm late class" she sticks the folder down and ties her hair back "I believe we have a new student with us?" She looks around and stops at me and opens her folder and reads the first page "Amy Thomas?" I smile and wave "that's me" she waves and nods "I am Miss Duncan" she grabs a book with a little girl holding a balloon on the front cover from her folder and walks towards me "welcome to my English class" she sticks the book in front of me and I smile "thank you" she looks at Ryder and raises her eyebrow "be nice to this one Mr James" Ryder rolls his eyes and leans back "I always am" the teacher scoffs and walks away towards her desk and sits down pulling her folder towards her. I look at Ryder and smile "what was that?" Ryder shrugs and leans forward looking towards Miss Duncan "her little sister fell in love with her and blames me for" he looks at me and smiles softly "never mind" he pulls his book out from his desk and opens it, I look at the teacher and see her going through her folder angrily "ok" I shake my head and look down towards my book before opening it and start to read it. The bell rings as I finish the 10th chapter and Miss Duncan walks towards me and smiles "how did we get on?" I close the book and stick it on my desk "good" I look towards the book and smile "I got too chapter 11" Ryder laughs nervously and shakes his head "what? I'm only on chapter 7 and I've been reading it for a week more than you" I laugh nervously and shrug "I'm a fast reader" Miss Duncan looks at Ryder and smirks "and you're a slow reader

Ryder" Ryder looks at her and rolls his hands "whatever" he stands up and grabs his bag "you coming Amy?" I smile and stand up "yeah" I grab my book and stick it in my bag "by kids" I smile at Miss Duncan before following Ryder out the classroom and walk down the hallway in silent. I follow Ryder towards the science hallway and he nods towards the doors "who's your science teacher?" I look at the doors and point towards the second left one "Mrs Luton" he smiles and nods "I'm in here so I will get you after class and we can go lunch?" I smile and nod "ok" I walk towards my classroom and look back and see Ryder smiling at me before heading into his classroom, I take a deep breath before walking into my classroom. I see a young-looking woman standing by the white board writing on it before looking towards me and stopping "you must be Amy?" I smile and nod walking towards her "yeah" she points towards the back of the class and smiles "the back lab desk is free so you can get set up there" she faces the white board again and starts writing "your work and books are already there for you and your lab partner won't be long I imagine" I walk towards the back of the class and sit on the stool and pull the folder on my desk forward and look through it. "Hey!" I look up and see Brody pulling the stool beside me out and he sits on it "hey" I smile at him softly before looking back towards the folder "you my new lab partner then?" I nod and smile sarcastically "looks like it" he moves forward and smirks "good" I look at him and raise my eyebrow "is it?" Brody smiles softly and looks towards the floor "are you still mad about my brother because I'm sorry about him" I take a deep breath and shake my head "no" he looks at me and shrugs "so what then?" I smile at him and shrug "nothing" he looks at me and smirks "good" I look at him and roll my eyes "so what have you been learning recently?" Brody pulls his notebook out and flicks through it "we have been mixing chemicals together and see what they do" I look at the box at the end of the desk and nod "so that's what that is" he smiles and moves the box in the middle of us and opens it pulling out ten jars of different colourful chemicals "just pick two and mix them together and see what they do then we write it down in the red book" he points towards my folder and I open it and take the red notebook out and place the folder at the end of the desk "let's see what these things can do then." Brody smiles and grabs a large jar from the box and places it in the middle before reaching down and grabbing safety goggles "here" I take the goggle and stick it on "I will go get us lap coats" he stands up and walks towards the front of the class "you don't have too!" I roll my eyes and grab two jars and stick one in the jar and stick the other one in "Amy not them!" I look at Brody and see him run towards me "what why?" Mrs Luton looks over and quickly stands up "everyone get out!" The class all start running towards the door and I look at the jar and see it starting too bubble and the chemicals start too rise up the jar "Amy get down!" Brody tackles me towards the ground as the jar fills up to the top and explodes "are you ok?" I hear the jar smash and feel the liquid touch my ankle "yeah" he looks up and nods "I think It's ok now" I look up and see smoke above us "stay down and cover your mouth" I look around the smoky classroom and nod "ok" I shake my head as I cover my mouth "why hasn't the smoke alarms went yet?" Brody smiles and points towards the ceiling and the smoke alarm starts ringing and I nod "bit slow" Brody pulls his jumper up over his mouth and stands up "come on" he holds his hands out and I take his hands and he pulls me up and grabs his jacket "here" he wraps it around me and covers my mouth and nose with it "let's go" he grabs our bags before heading towards the door and opening it. I head out the door and Brody closes it behind him "sorry about that" he shakes his head and rubs my arm "I'm just glad you're ok" I look towards my ankle and shake my head "I think I got a bit of chemical on my ankle because It's starting to sting" he bends down towards my ankle and rubs it "we should get it looked at" I laugh nervously and shake my head "what?" He smiles softly and shrugs "it will be nothing but just in case" I take a deep breath and nod "ok." He points down the hallway and I start walking down it "Miss Thomas!" I turn around and see Mrs Luton walking towards us "principles office now!"

Brody shakes his head and steps forward "she was just heading too" Mrs Luton shakes her head "I don't care where she was heading" she looks at me and crosses her arms "she nearly blew the school up so I'm not going to ask you again" I rub Brody's arm and smile "I will go after" Brody smiles and nods "ok" I walk down the hallway after Mrs Luton and she walks towards the principal's office and opens the door for me "she's waiting for you" I walk in and see an older woman sitting behind the desk "have a seat Miss Thomas" I sit down and look towards the floor "I believe you nearly set the school on fire? And on your first day" I laugh nervously and look at her "I'm sorry I didn't know what they would do" she smiles softly and nods "you wouldn't believe how many new students have been sent here because of that situation" she shakes her head and stands up "It's not your fault" she hands me a piece of paper and nods "but be more careful in future and don't do anymore chemical mixers without your lab partner behind there understood?" I nod firmly and smile "yes it won't happen again" she smiles and nods firmly "ok good to hear that" she points towards the door and smiles softly "thank you for coming in and welcome too Flathead High School" I smile and stand up "thank you" I walk towards the door closing it behind me. I walk towards the bathroom and see Abbie in there with two of her friends laughing but stop when she spots me and fix's her lipstick in the mirror "yeah me and Ryder will get back together soon and I will not let anything or anyone stop that" she looks at me in the mirror as I get into a toilet cubical and close it behind me. "You are Ryder are so cute and youse will look cute at the end of school year dance next Friday" Abbie finishes her lipstick and places it back in her pocket before making a kissing face towards the mirror "I know" she walks towards the bathroom door with her friends following behind her. I take a deep breath when I hear the bathroom door close behind them "thank god!" I walk out the cubical and walk towards the wash base and wash my hands and look in the mirror and fixing my hair "ouch!" I look towards my ankle as it stings and spot blood dripping down my ankle and onto my clean white trainers "what?" I grab a paper towel and bend down and clean my ankle and see a white scar, I grab another paper towel and wet it and bend down towards my ankle and clean it. I take a deep breath and stand back up and stick the paper towels in the bin before heading towards the door and pull it open but it doesn't move so I try push it "hello?" I try again and shake my head "I'm in here! Can anyone hear me?" I fling my head back and sigh "great" I look around and laugh nervously "of course Brody has my bag and phone" I bang on the door a few times and hear a bang from the other side "Amy?" I smile when I hear Brody's voice from the other side "Brody? I'm in the girl's bathroom" I bang the door again and smile "why is it locked?" I laugh nervously and shrug "I don't know" after a few silent seconds I hear him laugh "ok step back" I roll my eyes and step back "there's no way you will break the door" the door comes in unbroken and Brody stands at the other side of "down" he smirks and shrugs "you were saying?" I smirk and roll my eyes "my mistake" he hands me my bag and smiles "I came to find you too give you this" I take it and stick it on my back "thank you." He starts to walk down the hallway "let's go" 34i follow him and we walk towards the cafeteria "let's eat" I smile and follow him towards a table with a few other boys and he sits down and points towards the free seat across from him "this is Amy everyone" everyone smiles towards me and I wave "hey" the boy next too Brody smirks and leans forward "so how do you know my boy Brody here?" He taps Brody's back and I smile "I'm his new neighbour" the boy smirks and looks me up and down "you moved into the old creepy spy's house" I look at Brody and raise my eyebrow "the what?" Brody looks at the boy and shakes his head "that's enough Noah" the boy looks at me and shrugs before leaning back "sorry" I smile softly and look down "I should go" Brody looks at me and smiles "where?" I smile and look at him "I should call Roxy and let her know how my first day is going" I grab my bag and stand up "nice meeting youse" I wave before walking towards the exit "nice" Brody looks at Noah and rolls his eyes "sorry I didn't know she didn't know" Brody looks back towards me and smiles "I haven't told her yet." I walk towards the hallway and look around when I'm out of sight "now where is the library" I look around and spot the sign for the library "bingo!" I walk towards the library and open the door and walk into the empty library "hello can I help you?" I see a woman behind the desk at the side of the library "where can I find books or newspapers about events that have happened in this town?" The woman gets out from behind the desk and points towards a bookshelf "here" she points towards a few books and smiles "do you know what event you are looking for?" I look at the books and nod slowly "the spy's who lived here?" The woman chokes and laughs nervously "the spy's who lived in the little black house?" I shrug and smile "yeah them" she grabs a book and hands me it "here you go" the bell rings and she smile "take it with you" I smile and stick it in my bag "thank you" I head towards the door and the woman heads back towards the desk "do you need a plaster?" I turn around and raise my eyebrows "what?" She nods towards my ankle "that looks sore" I look towards it and see try blood on my shoe "no I will be ok" she shrugs and smiles "ok." I walk out the door and walk towards the next class "Amy!" I turn around and see Noah running towards me "did you just come out the library?" I smile nervously and nod "yeah I had to get a book for something" he shakes his head and smirks "oh" he coughs and stands up straight "anyway I was wondering if you had a date for the End of school year dance next Friday?" I smile softly and shake my head "I don't know what that is so no" he runs his hand through his hair and laughs nervously "ok good so you can come with me" he shrugs and smiles softly "if you like?" I shrug and take a deep breath "I don't think I will be going sorry but thanks for asking" he smiles and nods "ok but if you change your mind then let me know" he grabs a piece of paper from his pocket and smirks handing me it "bye" he runs of down the hallway and I look at the paper and see his name and number "what a first day" I stick the piece of paper in my pocket before walking down the hallway. The rest of the day fly's in and after History I meet Brody outside "you want a ride home?"

I shake my head and smile "no I'm good" he looks around the car park and shakes his head "doesn't your cousin have an interview?" I raise my eyebrow and smirk "how do you know?" he smirks and shrugs "Roxy told Jeremy about it" I roll my eyes and walk down the stairs "I don't mind the walk" Brody runs down after me "It's a 5 mile walk" I smirk and get my earphones from my pocket and stick them in "sorry can't hear you" I run of down the road leaving Brody behind "Amy wait!" Brody bends down and picks up a piece of paper and looks at it "Noah!" He looks around and shakes his head before sticking the piece of paper in his pocket and walking towards his motorbike. I walk into my gate and see Brody's motorbike in his yard already and walk towards my house and open my front door "Roxy?!" I close the door behind me and stick my keys in the key bowl on the table by the front door and take my jacket of and hang it up before heading into the kitchen and grab an apple and walk towards the sink and wash it looking out the window I see Brody outside his back yard with another girl laughing and speaking looking very close and I can't help but scoff and turn the water of before biting into my apple and head upstairs into my room. I take my shoes of and flinging my bag onto my bed before grabbing a pair of clean joggers and sitting on the bed opening my bag and taking the book from the library out it and start reading it but stop when I hear someone come up the stairs "Amy?!" I smile and stick the book down "in here!" Roxy walks in and smiles "how was school?" I place the book under my pillow and sit up "well" I laugh nervously and shrug "I nearly burned the school down on my third class but yeah other than that it was fine" she laughs softly and shakes her head "why what happened?" I smirk and nod towards my window "we was too mix two chemicals together and see what they done but I must have mixed two bad ones and it exploded" I look down and smile "good job Brody was there or I could have been burned all over" I rub my ankle and shrug "but I did manage to burn my ankle" she looks towards it and smiles "looks like a red love heart tattoo" I look at it and smile "so it does" she stands up and looks around "I'm going to make dinner soon so let me know what you want" I lean back and smile "ok" she smiles and heads out the room closing the door slightly behind her. I grab my book and continue reading a few more pages but jump when I hear something hit of my window "Amy?!" I shake my head and quickly stand up "Brody?" I look out the window and see Brody hanging out his window "what are you doing?" He holds a piece of paper up and laughs nervously "what are YOU doing more like" I look at the paper and shake my head "what is that?" he flings it to the ground below and scoffs "It's Noah's number" I take a deep breath and smirk "I didn't ask for it he just gave me it" Brody laughs softly "oh" he runs his hand through his hair "are you drunk?" He stands up straight and shakes his head "no!" I roll my eyes and stand up straight "sober up Brody" I close the window and he smirk "bye Amy" I wave before closing my curtains and head back towards my bed "no more distractions" I grab my earphones and stick them into my phone and play music before grabbing the book and reading the rest of it. I finish the book and stick my earphones out and shake my head "wow" I look around and smile, I stick the book back into my bag and run downstairs "Roxy?" I look into the kitchen and see Roxy fixing up burgers "I was just going to call on you" I smile and she nods towards the table "thank you" I sit down and she places the plate and hands me a can of cola "so I got the job" I open my can and take a sip "I was going to ask how you got on" she smiles and nods "I start tomorrow morning" I nod and smile "well done you" she smirks and sits down "thank you." She laughs nervously and bites into her burger "what was you doing upstairs that was so quiet then?" I smile and take a bite out of the burger "I found a book about these spy's" she laughs nervously and takes a sip of her cola "the ones who used to live here?" I nod and smile "you know about them?" She scoffs and bite her burger "you really think I would move into a house without knowing the history of it all?" I shrug and smile "so why didn't you tell me? Everyone in my school knows about it so I got a book out and that's what I was doing upstairs" I eat another bite of burger and she smiles "what did the book say?" I look around and smile "that the spy's build at least 2 hidden rooms in the house and there's a panic room somewhere?" Roxy smiles and nods "what else?" I shrug and smile "not much really" I look at her and smile "mostly about them personally and how they was both spy's who fell in love while on a job and got married and lived here and Harry build the hidden rooms and a panic room because they took down one of the top drug lords and wanted to protect his wife Sharon" Roxy smiles and eats another bite of her burger "well that was 20 years ago and the house has been gone over hundreds of times and there's no sign of secret rooms or a panic room so It's probably a lot of rubbish that the spy's told because they got fired after" I smile softly and nod "after the started making up false stories about the town" Roxy smiles and nods "exactly so don't worry about it I'm sure It's all just tattle tales." I finish my burger and shrug "maybe so but It's just cool to think that there is hidden rooms in this house that we don't know about" I stand up and wash my plate "yeah well don't get all obsessed with her" Roxy stands up and walks towards me smiling "I know what you can get like" I roll my eyes and smile "I won't don't worry" she taps my back and nods "good" she walks towards the door and grabs her car keys "I'm going out so don't wait up" I walk towards the door and smirk "with who?" She looks down and blushes "Jeremy" I raise my eyebrow and laugh sarcastically "next door Jeremy" she rolls her eyes and opens the door "yes" she blows me a kiss and smirks "don't wait up" she closes the door behind her and I shake my head "I won't don't worry." I grab a bottle of water from the fridge and lock the front door before heading upstairs and into bed "empty house means early night" I smile and get under covers before closing my eyes and drifting off to sleep.

I wake up when I hear a loud bang from outside "Amy?!" I jump out of bed and run towards Roxy's room "Roxy!?" She runs out her room and hugs me "are you ok?" I hug her and nod "yeah what was that?" Roxy looks towards the front door "I don't know but stay here and I'll check it out" she walks down the stairs and I lean over them and look towards the front door as Roxy goes to open it there's another bang making me jump and scream "run!" she runs upstairs and I run into my bedroom and she follows me and we hide in my bathroom "it sounds like gunshots" she locks the bathroom door and looks out the window "stay down" I hide in the bath and she continues to look out the window "I think It's ok now" she walks towards the door but stops "someone's here" she looks around and grabs the toilet plunger and walks towards the bathroom door and jumps when it kicks in and runs towards it hitting something behind the door "ouch!" She looks towards the floor and drops the plunger "are you ok?" I get out the bathtub and walk towards the door "did you get them?" I look towards the floor and see Brody lying unconscious "is that Brody?" I walk towards my sink and soak a sponge in cold water and clean up the blood running down his face "let's try get him on my bed" I grab his shoulders and Roxy grabs his feet and we manage to lift him and place him on my bed "I will go get water and you stick the sponge on his head" I run back into the bathroom and soak the sponge under cold water and sit on the bed next to him sticking the sponge on his head. "I will be back in a minute" I nod and smile "ok" she runs of out the room and I look at Brody's unconscious face and smile running my hand down his face making him move and slowly open his eyes "hey you" I smile as he opens his eyes "no!" He quickly jumps up and looks around "Amy?" He looks me up and down and smiles "Amy!" He runs towards me and cuddles me "are you ok?" I smile and nod "I'm fine" Roxy runs in holding an ice bag and smiles "he's awake then" I jump back and smile "yeah" he rubs his head and laughs nervously "what did you hit me with?" She nods towards the bathroom and he spots the plungers on the floor "sorry about that" he smiles and shakes his head "It's fine." I look at him and shake my head "what are you doing here anyway?" He smiles and rubs my arm "I heard you scream so I ran in too see what happened" Roxy smirks and walks towards us "that's nice of you" she looks at me and shrugs "we heard a loud bang and thought we heard gunshots so we ran into the bathroom for cover" Brody runs his hand through his hair and laughs nervously "that was me sorry" he nods towards the window and smirks "I was fixing my motorbike and it backfired sorry" Roxy shakes her head and walks out the room "I'm going back to bed since we are not under attack" I laugh nervously and wave "night." I look back at Brody and smile "why are you fixing your bike at" I look at my alarm clock and shake my head "4AM?" He sits down on my bed and shrugs "can't sleep and I like fixing things when I'm stressed or had a bad day" I smile softly and sit next to him "want to talk about it?" He smiles softly and looks at me "I should get back and get sleep" he stands up and I nod "are you sure? Your more than welcome to stay for a while?" He smirks and looks at my bed "no I will let you get some rest" he smiles and waves "I will let myself out" I smile softly and nod "ok" he walks towards my bedroom door and I sit down on the bed when I hear the front door close behind him. I lie down on bed and close my eyes for a few minutes before sitting back up "yip that's me wide awake" I stand up and walk downstairs and grab a bottle of water from the fridge and look out the back window and see Brody in his shed sticking tools back, he looks over and smirks waving "hi" I wave back and he walks towards his back door and disappears. I smile and shake my head "bedtime" I walk upstairs and head into bed and fall asleep as soon as I close my eyes. The next morning, I run downstairs and grab a slice of toast from the table "morning" I run out the door and wave "bye" I grab my keys and open the front door "wait!" I look behind me and Roxy runs after me "you not want a ride?" I look at the clock and shake my head "haven't you got work?" She smiles and nods "yes but I don't start until 9:30 so I have time to drive you" I smile and nod "ok" she grabs her jacket and follows me out closing the door behind her. I get into the car and smile at Roxy "so are you excited about starting a new job?" Roxy looks at me and smiles "yes I can't wait" I smile and nod "you will smash it" she looks at me and nods "thank you." She pulls up outside the school and parks "I will drop you of here" she laughs nervously and shrugs "don't want people to know your cousin drops you of" I grab my bag and smirk

"It's ok you're a cool cousin" she shoves me and laughs softly "get out of here kiddo before you go soft" I smile and nod "good luck" I open the car door and she smiles and waves "you too" I close the door behind me and she drives of. I walk towards the school entrance and see Ryders motorbike pull up and he waves as he parks "Amy!" I turn around and look towards him "wait up!" He takes his helmet of and run towards me smiling "hey" I smile and wave "hi" he looks towards the school and smiles "want me to walk you too class? We have English first anyways" I smile and nod "ok then" we walk towards the school entrance and I spot Brody by his locker speaking too Noah looking frustrated and looks towards me when I walk in and smiles "so how was your first day anyway?" I smile and nod "it was good" he smiles and nods "good" I look towards the ground as we walk down the rest of the hallway and I look up when I see a shadow next to me "Amy?" I look up and see Brody smiling "can I speak to you for a second?" I nod and smile "yeah" he looks at Ryder and smirks "in private?" Ryder rolls his eyes and takes a deep breath "I will be over by my locker" he walks towards a locker a few feet away and Brody smiles "how you feeling?" I shrug and smile "ok" I look towards his head and smirk "how's your head" he rubs it and laughs softly "I thought it was a dream when I woke up this morning until I felt it and realised it was bruised" I smirk and look down "sorry about that" he shrugs and runs his hand through his hair "It's fine I'm sure Roxy didn't mean to hit me personally" I smile and shake my head "she felt bad about it" he shrugs and laughs softly "tell her not too." He stands up straight and nods towards Noah "so you and Noah?" I look towards him and laugh nervously "what?" He smiles and looks down "he said that he gave you his number" I feel my pockets and laugh nervously "so he did" I shake my head and look towards Noah "I forgot about that" I take a deep breath and shrug "I lost it anyway but no I'm going for a drama free year which includes boys" he looks at me and smirks "too bad." I blush and feel my legs go weak a little "anyway I should go" I cough and nod "ok" he nods towards Ryder and smirks "let you get back too pretty boy over there" I look towards Ryder and smile "be careful your starting to sound jealous" he walks backwards and smirks towards me "would that be such a bad thing?" I laugh nervously and shake my head "wait what?" my face drops and he winks and turns around. Ryder walks back towards me and laughs sarcastically "what did he want?" I smile and shake my head "just asked about Noah because he gave me his number yesterday" Ryder looks towards Noah and smirks "really?" I smile and shrug "yeah but I lost it so I told him not to worry" Ryder looks at me and smiles "so you and Brody?" I roll my eyes and shove him softly "me and no one" I walk down the hallway and looks back towards Brody and looks him up and down before walking down the hallway and catching up with me. After English I have P.E so I walk towards the gym but get lost and see a girl standing by the gym door "can you tell me where the girls changing room is?" She smirks and nods "the second door on the right" I look down the hallway and smile "thank you" I walk down the hallway and Abbie approaches the girl and smirks "what did she want?" The girl laughs sarcastically "directions to the girls changing room" I walk into the door on the second right and Abbie laughs "but that's the boys changing room" the girls looks at Abbie and shrugs "oops" they both laugh and walk towards the second door on the left. I go into my school bag as I walk into the changing room and walk towards a locker and stick it in before turning around and seeing a bunch of half-naked boys, I freeze and my face goes bright red as they all laugh "Amy?" Brody walks out from the crowd and I shrug "I got told this was the girls changing room" the boys continue to laugh and I shake my head and run out the changing room "Amy wait!" Brody quickly sticks on his joggers and runs towards the door but stop when he spots my bag in the locker "not ok guys" the boys stop laughing and look towards the ground as Brody grabs my bag and runs out the door and runs after me. I run down the hallway and into the girl's toilets and into a cubical "Amy?" I shake my head and look up "go away" he slides my bag under the cubical and smiles softly "ok but it could have been worse" I stand up and open the door "how?" He looks at me and smirks "you couldn't have seen my half naked" I roll my eyes and smirk "your such a dork" he hugs me and smiles "I know but least I got you too smile" I hug him and he picks my bag up "here" I take it and he shoves me "let's skip P.E" he shrugs and smiles "I know this great little pizza place" I smile and nod "ok" he laughs softly and shakes his head "really?" I roll my eyes and shove him softly "yes dork" I walk towards the bathroom door and he follows "ok well let me just grab my bag and I will meet you outside?" I smile and nod "ok" he walks towards the changing room and turns around and laughs softly "don't try follow me now" I roll my eyes and shake my head "I will try" I smirk and walk towards the school exit doors.

After a few minutes Brody comes out and smiles "ready? I smile and nod and follow him towards the car park "here" he hands me his helmet and I take a deep breath "can we not walk?" He smirks and shakes his head "no" I roll my eyes and get on the back of the bike "fine" he drives of towards the town centre and stops outside a little pizza place "I used to come here every Friday with Jeremy and my parents he smiles softly and I rub my arm "well we can come here every Friday if you like?" He smirks and nods "I would love that" I walk towards the door and open it "good. Now let's go because I am hungry" he follows me in and we sit down at a table "you want a cola?" I nod and smile "yes please" he stands up and walks towards the counter and gets 2 colas and walks back towards me "thank you" I take the can and take a sip and pick up the menu. "What do you fancy?" I look at him and smirk "pizza" he rolls his eyes and looks at me "what pizza?" I smile and stick the menu down "anything chicken" he sticks his menu down and nods "ok" he stands up and walks towards the counter and comes back "won't be long" I smile and sit up straight "what did you order me" he winks and leans back "pizza" I roll my eyes and lean back "funny." After our pizza comes out he smiled at me and nods towards my lips "what?" He shakes his head and hands me a napkin "you have a little something" I take the napkin and dab my face and see a bit of cheese hang from my nose "oh god" he smirks and licks his lips "you got it" I roll my eyes and laugh softly "good." He smiles and looks down towards his pizza "so what made you and Roxy travel?" I laugh nervously and shake my head "Roxy wanted too" I look down too avoid eye contact and he nods "so where have youse been?" I look up and smile "everywhere" he laughs sarcastically and nods slowly "I've only ever been too New York with my dad one time when he had this huge law case and had to go there for the week" I look at him and smile softly "was it nice?" He looks at me and nods "was lovely but too busy" he looks around and shrugs "I prefer a nice quiet town where nothing happens but New York you hear sirens and It's too loud" I look down and nod "it is a busy city." After pizza he walks towards the counter and hands the woman his bank card and I shake my head "I will get next one" he smirks and looks into my eyes "does that mean there will be a next time?" I smile and look down blushing "yeah" he takes his bank card back and smiles "good." I walk towards the door and he hands me his helmet and gets on the bike "we will get back just before lunch finishes" I smile and get on the back of his bike "good because I don't think I can handle looking at another piece of food" he smirks and looks back towards me and smirks "don't look at me then" I roll my eyes and slap him softly "just drive" he laughs softly and drives towards school. We get back to school as the bell goes and he smiles and gets of "told you" he helps me of and I smile. I look towards the school and shake my head "thank god we are halfway through the day already" I walk towards the school entrance and he follows. I spot Ryder at his locker and he looks over towards us and looks Brody up and down before slamming his locker shut and walking down the hallway "think someone is in the bad books" I roll my eyes and walk towards my locker "I'm really not in the mood for boy drama right now" Brody follows me and smiles "are you like of boys completely?" I look at him and smirk opening my locker "yes" he shrugs and leans against the locker next to me "forever?" He leans closer towards me and I can feel his hands by mine "yes" I slam my locker and he jumps and follows me down the hallway "shame" I look at him and smirk "for you maybe." He takes a deep breath and flings his head back "maybe" I smile and shake my head "have you not go a girlfriend anyway?" I stop outside my maths class and smile at him "no?" I roll my eyes and walk in backwards "I see you with that girl" he smiles and shakes his head "when?" I shrug and look him up and down "yesterday" he smirks and licks his lips "you best watch you sound jealous" I roll my eyes and turn around "bye Brody" he looks at me and takes a deep breath "she isn't my girlfriend" he shakes his head and sighs before walking towards his class. I walk towards the back of the class and see Ricky smiling towards me "what?" He shrugs and smiles "have fun with Brody?" I roll my eyes and sit down "It's not like that" he leans towards me and smiles "that's not what Ryder thinks" I take my jacket of and take a deep breath "I don't date and they both of them need to realise that" he smirks and leans back on his chair "have you made it clear that you don't?" I shrug and lean back "no" he laughs softly and shakes his head "maybe you should" he looks towards the front and I smile

"I know I will." After class I walk out and my phone rings and I see Roxy's name come up so I answer it "hey you are not in class are you?" I walk down the hallway and shake my head "just finished Maths why what's wrong?" I walk down the stairs and she takes a deep breath "they are keeping me on till later from tomorrow" I laugh softly and shake my head "and?" She laughs nervously and I smile "and you thought I couldn't take care of myself?" I scoff and walk towards the history department "no I just wanted to let you know" I stand outside history and smile "good well I will see you after work" I hang up and walk into class and sit down. We watch another movie during history so I yawn and rest my head on the desk when the history teacher turns the lights out and close my eyes drifting off to sleep the rest of the class. I wake up when the teacher turns the lights on and yawn sitting up "nice sleep" I look around and see Noah sitting beside me "yeah" he smirks and stands up "you snore by the way" he shakes his head and laughs softly before walking out the class "I do not" I smile nervously and walk out the classroom and towards music class but stop at the top of the stairs when I see Ryder and Brody at the bottom arguing "hey!" I run down the stairs and shake my head "what's going on here?" Brody shakes his head and pushes past me "nothing" he walks down the hallway and I look at Ryder "well?" He rolls his eyes and scoffs "forget it" he walks in the opposite direction leaving me standing there myself confused "boys!" I shake my head and sigh. The rest of the afternoon drags in and I look at the clock every 10 minutes until the bell finally rings and I quickly stand up and head out the door and towards the exit, I get outside and take a deep breath and walk down the stairs "Amy?" I turn around and see Brody and Noah walking out "wait up" Brody nods towards Noah and he runs of past me and smiles "bye" I nod and smile "bye Noah" I look at Brody and he smiles and runs down the stairs "sorry about earlier" I smile and shake my head "it's fine" I shrug and scoff "it wasn't my business to get involved" he smirks and looks down "right." He looks towards the car park and nods "your ride's here" I turn around as Roxy pulls up and beeps her horn "I should go" he smiles and nods "ok" I turn around and run towards Roxy's car leaving him standing there himself. I get into the car and take a deep breath "boy trouble?" I laugh nervously and shake my head "something like that" I stick my belt on and she looks towards Brody "want to talk about it?" I lean back and shake my head "I will when I know what to say" she laughs softly and drives of "well I am all ears when you are ready" I look at her and roll my eyes "oh I know" I smirk and shake my head "you will be the first one to know." She parks outside the house and I look towards Brody's house as I walk up the steps and see his front door open and the girl I seen before walk out and closing the door behind her before looking over towards me and smile, I walk into the house and close the door behind me. "Why is this house always so warm" Roxy shrugs and smiles "I don't know" I scoff and shake my head "I'm going to study" I run upstairs and into my room before Roxy can question me, I place my bag on my bed and open the window and see Brody in his room working out so I scoff before heading towards my bed and sitting down. I turn my TV on and flick through a few channels and take a deep breath and stand up, I walk towards my drawers and pick up my camera and run downstairs "I'm going out" Roxy pops her head out from the kitchen and smiles "where?" I show her my camera and smile "ok I will just order pizza when your back" I smile and nod "ok" I open the door and walk out closing it behind me. I look towards Brody's house as I pass it and shake my head before walking down the rest of the street fixing the settings on my camera, after a few seconds I bang into someone dropping the camera out my hand and towards the ground "wow there!" I see two hands grab my camera before it falls onto the ground "don't want you breaking that now do we" I look up and see a boy with bright green eyes smiling at me holding my camera "thank you" I take the camera and shake my head "I would be lost without this" he smirks showing of amazing white teeth "your welcome." He looks into my eyes for a few seconds before shaking his head and laughing nervously "so what you taking pictures of?" I smile and look at my camera "not sure yet" I look around and shrug "not sure what this town has to offer yet" he nods firmly and smiles "I know the perfect place if you like forests and you might even spot a few wildlife animals?" I smile and nod "that would be perfect" he looks at his watch and shakes his head "I have time it's fine" he walks back down the street and smiles "come on" I follow him down the street and he stops a few meters down and points up an of road path that leads into the woods "follow the path and in a few meters you will see the most amazing forest and in a few more meters you will see a waterfall and lake where the animals usually go if your quiet enough" I smile and nod "thank you" he looks at his watch again and smiles "I should go" I cough and stand up straight "ok" I smile and walk up the of road path "thank you" he smile and waves "your welcome" he walks back up the street and I turn around and walk into the woods. After a few feet I hear a branch snap from behind me "change your mind?" I turn around and see a little brown puppy sitting down looking towards me "hey there little guy" he wags his tail and I smile "come here" I bend down and the puppy runs towards me and licks my hand "what are you doing out here all alone?" I look around and shake my head "no collar?" I pick it up and smile "yip definitely a boy" I stick him back down and smile "what are we going to do with you?" I look around and smile "that boy said there is a lake around here so we could get you a drink" I shake my head and take a deep breath "but I bet your hungry huh?" He barks and wags his tail "take that as a yes" I smile and nod "come on then" I walk back towards the street and the puppy follows me "let's get you some food and water" he looks up the street and stops "what's wrong boy?" I see a large ginger cat sitting on a fence a few feet in front of us "it's ok boy" the puppy doesn't move so I smile and shake my head "come on then" I pick him up and he licks my face and I shake my head and wipe it "thanks for that" I walk down the street and close my gate behind us "there you go pal" I stick him down and smile "come on" I walk up the stairs and he follows "you ready for this?" He barks and I take a deep breath "let's do this" I open the door and the dog runs in and runs into the kitchen and I hear Roxy scream "here goes nothing" I close the door behind me and walk into the kitchen. "Only me" I smile and she shakes her head "what is that doing here?" I roll my eyes and grab two small bowls "be nice" I fil a bowl up with water "I found him in the woods and I didn't want to leave him there" I stick the bowl of water down and fill the other bowl with bits of meat "he can't stay here" the dog runs towards the food and eats it "why not?" She laughs nervously and shakes her head "where is he going to sleep? You don't have anything for it" I roll my eyes and sit down "he can sleep in my room and I have some money in my piggy bank so I will go get him stuff" she rolls her eyes and takes a deep breath "fine" she shakes her head and smiles "but he is your dog so your responsibly" he turns around before doing a poo "which means you look and clean after him and walk him" I take a deep breath and nod "I will." I smirk and grab a sheet of kitchen roll and pick it up "see?" I walk towards the front door and stick it in the bin outside and walk back into the kitchen "I will go to the mall now and get things for him" I look towards him and see him sleeping next to the bowls "and he needs a name" Roxy looks towards him and smirks "Tramp?" I roll my eyes and walk towards the stairs "no." I run upstairs and grab my piggy bank and empty it on my bed and grab the money that falls out and stick it in my purse "that should be enough" I run back downstairs and see Roxy grabbing the blanket from the sofa "you want me to drive you?" I nod and smile "yeah" he walks back into the kitchen and sticks the blanket down and lifts the puppy onto it "there" I smile and she shakes her head "what?" I shrug and laugh softly "nothing." We drive to the mall and she looks at it "is there even a pet place here?" I shrug and get out the car "there should be something" she gets out the car and we walk towards the entrance "oh look there's Brody" I look over and see Brody standing with the girl from earlier. Roxy waves towards him and he waves back and smiles "what's he done now?" I shake my head and look down "nothing" she raises her eyebrow and shakes her head "jealous?" I scoff and shake my head "definitely not" I look over towards him before entering the mall. We walk towards the stairs and I see a little girl not older than 2 walking about on her own heading for the stairs "wow!" I run towards her and lift her up as she is about to take a step down the first stair making her cry "hey shh you're ok" I smile at her and she cuddles into me "you ok?" She looks at me and laughs "now let's find your parents" I look around and see a man holding a pink bag "is that your daddy?" The little girl looks towards the man and smiles "daddy!" The man looks towards me and smiles "Lola!" He runs towards me and takes a deep breath "sorry about her" I hand him her and smile "it's fine I'm just glad I got her before she tried to go down the stairs" he looks towards the stairs and takes a deep breath "she did?" I smile softly and nod "yeah" he grabs his wallet from his pocket and hands me money "I don't want your money" he shakes his head and looks me up and down "then at least take my card? If you need a job my garage is in town so keep it?" I smile and he hands me a card "ok" I stick the card in my pocket and look towards the little girl "you be good for your daddy" the little girl smiles and nods "ok." The man holds his hand out and smiles "Craig" I shake his hand and smile "Amy" he pulls his hand away and nods "thank you again" he grabs the pink bag and smile "your welcome" he waves and walks towards the exit "bye" I wave and smile "bye" he disappears and Roxy walks towards over towards me "you working in a garage?" I look at her and shrug "I don't know anything about cars but it would be rude not to take his card" she smiles and nods "he just wants to see you covered in oil" I shove her softly and scoff "let's go." We walk down the stairs and I nod towards a home store "there should be something in there" Roxy shakes her head and points down the mall "I'm guessing the pet store will be a better call?" I smile and nod "yeah probably" we walk towards the pet store and Roxy grab a trolley and smiles "ok so what do we need?" I smirk and shrug "everything" she rolls her eyes and scoff "let's go then." We walk down the aisles and I pick up a bed and blanket "what about a cage?" I shake my head and walk past them "no it won't need one" Roxy laughs softly and shakes her head "ok well if he breaks anything while we are out then it's on you" I nod firmly and keep walking "fine." We walk down the food isle and I grab 2 bowls and look at the food "there's so many" I look at Roxy and shrug "how do I know what one too pick?" She smiles and shakes her head "you don't know it's age but it's definitely a puppy so puppy food would be a good idea" I nod and grab a box of puppy food and walk down the toy isle "toys" I grab a pack of tennis balls and stick them in the trolley and turn around when I feel someone touch my shoulder "hey you" I turn around and see Ryder with another girl holding a big bag of dog food. "Hi" I see Roxy smiling at the side of my eye "this is my cousin Roxy" he sticks the bag of food in the one hand and holds his other hand out "Ryder" she shakes his hand and smiles "nice too finally put a face to your name" Ryder looks at me and smirks "so what's been said about me? All good things I hope" he looks back towards her and she nods "of course" he smirks towards me and nods "this is my little sister Chloe" I smile at her and nod "nice to meet you" she smirks and nods "you too" she looks at Ryder and shrugs "eventually" Ryder's face goes red and I laugh softly "we should get going" he looks at my trolley and smiles "new dog?" I nod and smile "yeah" he smirks and nods "what's its name?" I look at Roxy and laugh nervously "we haven't actually given him a name yet" Ryder laughs softly and shakes his head "really?" I look at him and smirk "Bear" he smiles and nods "Bear is cute" Roxy shrugs and laughs softly "Bear it is then." Ryder waves and walks down the aisle "see you tomorrow" I smile and nod "see you tomorrow" I walk down the aisle and shake my head "don't even say anything" Roxy follows behind me and shakes her head "I wasn't going too." I pick up a few more toys and get a lead and collar and head towards the checkout and the woman scans the things and nods "$65 please" I laugh softly and look at Roxy "you can pay me back" she gets her card and hands it too the woman "thank you" I grab the bags and head towards the door and Roxy gets her card back and follows behind me. When we get back home I run towards the door and see Bear running towards me barking playfully "hey boy" I stroke him and smile "come on" I run upstairs and into my bedroom and place the bags on my bed "now where can we stick your bed?" Roxy walks in and shakes her head "here" she hands me another bag from the pet store and shrugs "dinner will be ready in an hour" I nod and smile "ok" she walks back out the room and I stick the dog bed at the side of mine and smile "there you go boy" Bear runs towards the bed and sniffs it before lying down "good boy." I look at the toys and shake my head before looking around my room "Roxy?!" I walk towards my door and see Roxy at the bottom of the stairs "what?" I smile and look at her "have we got an old box or something I can stick all his toys in?" She looks towards the living room and nods "yeah" she walks away and comes back a few seconds later holding an old looking magazine holder box "this do?" I smile and run downstairs "yes thank you" I take the box and run back towards my room and empty all the toys into it and stick it at the side of his bed. I attach his name tag on the collar and stick it around his neck "there you go" I smile and stroke him "Bear." I grab the bag with his food and treats and head to the kitchen "I'm going to stick Bears food in this cupboard ok?" I pour food and water into his bowl and place it by the back door before opening an empty cupboard and stick his food and treats in it "what you going to do next?" I turn around and shrug "what do you mean?" Roxy rolls her eyes and shakes her head "you need to take him to the vets and see if there is anything wrong with him" I laugh nervously and look down "what if he comes up in the system that he is someone else's dog?" Roxy scoffs and shakes her head "I thought you found him in the woods?" I nod and smile "I did" she cuts an onion and smirks "well there's a good chance he won't be and he's from a litter from a stray" I smile and nod "I hope so" I walk towards the door and look back "I like him" I turn around and walk up the stairs and see him sleeping still, I smile softly and close the door again before heading back downstairs "he's sleeping so I will leave him for now" Roxy nods and smiles "fine but you can take him tomorrow after school" I nod and smile "I will" she hands me a knife and smirks "you can help me chop" I roll my eyes and walk towards her "fine" I take the knife and start cutting the veg with her. After I cut my first carrot someone knocks on the front door and I hear Bear barking "I will get it" I walk towards the door and see Bear run down the stairs "it's ok boy" I open the door and see Ryder standing outside holding a bag "hey" he hands me the bag and I shake my head "what's this for?" He looks down and she smirks "I remember what it's like having a new pup so I got you a few things that helped me" I look in the bag and see a bear teddy "that's cute" I take it out and he smiles "glad you like it." Roxy walks towards the door and smiles "who is it?" I look back towards her and smile "Ryder" she smirks and shrugs "why don't you stay for dinner Ryder?" I raise my eyebrows and mouth "no" she walks towards the door and opens it "we have plenty for you" he looks at me and smiles "if you don't mind?" I shake my head and open the door "no I don't mind" he walks in and I shake my head towards Roxy and shove her softly. Ryder walks into the living room and I follow him "dinner will be ready in 20 mins" Ryder smiles and sits down "ok" I look towards Roxy and she shrugs "do you want a drink Ryder?" he looks at Roxy and shrugs "just give me anything" Roxy nods towards me and walks into the kitchen so I smile towards Ryder and nod "I will get it" I follow her into the kitchen and close the door slightly behind me. "What the hell Roxy" she grabs two cans of cola from the fridge and hands me it "oh lighten up" she smirks and shrugs "he seems nice" I roll my eyes and take the can's "I don't do boys remember? So cupid Roxy can stay in" I take a deep breath and nod "so how do I look?" Roxy smirks and pushes a strand of hair behind my ear "beautiful" I smile and hug her "thank you" I walk back into the living room and see Ryder on the sofa with Bear, I hand him a can of cola and sit down on the other sofa. "Thank you" I smile and open my can "so this is Bear?" he looks at Bear and I nod and take a sip "yeah that's him" he laughs softly and shakes his head "you know he's got dirt in his eyes and all over his stomach?" I look at him and shake my head "yeah he's been out the back all morning" I laugh nervously and take another sip of my cola "Roxy?!" Roxy walks in and looks towards Ryder "how long till dinner?" Roxy looks at her clock and smiles "15 mins" Ryder looks at me and smirks "perfect" he stands up and lifts Bear "enough time for us to give him a bath" I shake my head and smiles "us?" He nods and walks towards me "yeah come in" he walks upstairs and I shrug towards Roxy and follow him "where's the bathroom?" I nod towards my room door and he walks in it "if you wanted me in your room all you had to do was ask" he smirks and I roll my eyes and walk towards my ensuite bathroom and open the door "oh" he laughs nervously and walks towards the shower and turns it on "come on buddy let's get you washed." He sticks Bear in the bath and smiles toward me "you just going to stand there or you coming to help?" I smile and walk towards him and bend down "I will help." He scrubs Bear and I watch all the dirt go down the drain hole "there's a good boy" he stops scrubbing him and Bear barks and shakes making the water go all over Ryder's top making it soak "thanks for that buddy" Bear barks and Ryder stands up and shakes his head looking towards me "you don't have a spare top I could wear do you?" I stand up and nod "I will check." I walk into my bedroom and grab a jumper from my drawers "here" he walks out from the bathroom with no t-shirt on carrying Bear wrapped in a towel like a baby "wow" he looks at me and smirks "what?" I shake my head and look down towards the floor nervously "nothing" he sits on the bed and dry's Bear and I smile and sit next to him "here" I hand him the jumper and smile "this should fit you" he sits Bear next to him and stands up "thank you." He stands in front of the window and I look at him as he sticks the jumper on "help!" It gets stuck halfway and I smirk and shake my head "ok stay still and I will get it" I stand up and walk towards him "here" I pull the jumper down and he shakes his head and laughs nervously "I wanted it of" I look down and smile softly "oh" he looks down towards the jumper and smirks "guess me keeping it is another excuse to come over and see you" I push a strand of hair behind me ear and smirk "why would you need an excuse? Roxy said I can have friends over whenever I want" he rolls his eyes and leans forward "good" I look up and see his eyes locked onto my lips and he licks his before moving in and kissing me. His lips are soft and nice, it was the best kiss I had. I hadn't kissed a lot of boys but this was one of the best and I didn't want it to stop. "Amy!" I bite Ryders lip and jump back "sorry" I look around and see Brody hanging out his window looking into mine "hey Brody" I laugh nervously and walk towards my window "what's up?" He looks at Ryder and shakes his head "just wanted to check on you after today but I can see you are fine" I look down and smirk "thank you" he rolls his eyes and scoffs "whatever" he looks at Ryder and shakes his head "stay away from me" he slams his window shut and closes his curtains "awkward" Ryder looks at me and shrugs "what was that about?" I take a deep breath and close my window "no idea" I turn around towards Ryder and he forces a smile "I should go" I smile and shake my head "what? No, you have to stay for dinner. Roxy will kill me if she think's I have scared her dinner guest away" he smirks and nods "ok" he walks towards me and takes my hand and kisses it "let's go downstairs" he walks towards the door and I take a deep breath and shake my head "this is going to be one awkward dinner" I help Bear of the bed and walk towards the door with Bear following behind me. I walk into the kitchen and see Ryder placing plates on the table "I can do that" Ryder smirks and shakes his head "no that's fine" I shrug and smile "ok" I sit down at the table and he hands me a can of cola and smirks "thank you." Roxy comes over carrying a large dish of mac and cheese and sticks it in the middle of the table "help yourself" I stick a portion on the plates and Ryder sits next to me and smirks "thanks" he looks at his plate and nods "this looks amazing Roxy" Roxy sits down and smiles "thank you" she eats a mouthful of the food and he looks at me and smiles before eating into his. After dinner Ryder stands up and places the plates in the sink "I can do that" Roxy stands up and he shakes his head "no you made the dinner so let me clean up" she looks at me and smirks "I like him" I roll my eyes and stand up "I'm going to wash my hands and get this cheese smell of" I walk upstairs and head into my bathroom. "So what's your plan with my cousin?" Roxy smirks and hands Ricky another fork "I'm not sure I have one" he looks at her and shrugs "just go with it I guess" Roxy shakes her head and smiles "that's the best way but it will probably backfire" Ryder raises his eyebrow and Roxy laughs softly "I hope not." I walk out from the bathroom and feel a cold breeze coming in so I walk towards my window and close it and see Brody in his room working out and I stand there for a few seconds and just stare into his room and look at his large biceps going tense every time he does a push up on his bars, I gulp and feel my lips start too rise into a smile "hey!" I jump and turn around and see Ryder standing by my room door "hey you" I quickly close the curtains and walk towards him "can we sit here for a few minutes?" He nods towards my bed and I smile and nod "of course" I sit down and he joins me and looks down smiling "so" he looks at me and takes a deep breath "I would like to get to know you a bit better" I smile and nod slowly "Ryder I" he touches my hand and shakes his head "don't shoot me down yet" he stands up and smirks "think about it and let me know over dinner? Say this

Saturday?" I scoff and nod "dinner sounds good" he smirks and nods "ok good" he steps back and nods "I'm going to go now but give it a good think through" I look down and laugh nervously "I will" he nods and smirks "good" he disappears out the door and I shake my head and lie back onto the bed "what am I doing?" I sit up and grab a book from my school bag and start reading it and get four chapters in when Roxy walks into my room "can I come in?" I stick the book under my pillow and nod "yeah." She walks in and sits next to me handing me a bar of chocolate "want to tell me what happened?" I take the chocolate and open it "don't know what you're talking about" I shrug and eat into the chocolate and she folds her legs on the bed and laughs softly "you read when your either stressed or have a problem that you can't solve" I smirk and grab the book from under my pillow and nod "just things" she smiles and looks down "Ryder you mean?" I stick the book back and lay back on the bed "maybe" she stands up and smiles "well you want my advice?" I sit up straight and nod "always" she laughs softly and nods "he's a good one" she walks towards the door and looks back before exiting "and your motto has gone down the drain." I roll my eyes and eat the last bit of my chocolate "was a stupid motto anyway I'm not a nun!" I smirk and grab my book before leaning back and reading the rest of it.

When I finally finish the book, I yawn and take a deep breath 'what time is it?' I check my phone and smile '11PM?' I shake my head and stand up and walk into the hallway "Roxy?" I see her bedroom light of but her room door wide open "Roxy?!" I look downstairs and run down them looking into the living room "hello!" I head into the kitchen and see Bear sitting by the back-door barking "hey boy" I walk towards the door and see a shadow walking out the back garden "come on boy!" I pick Bear up and stick him in the living room "stay here." I close the door behind me and look upstairs "Roxy?!" I shake my head and take a deep breath and look back into the kitchen and out the window "what?" I shake my head and laugh nervously "Roxy?" I walk towards the window and see Roxy sleepwalking "not again!" I run towards the back door and open it and run towards her laughing softly "what are you doing?" Still closing her eyes she walks towards the fence in-between mine and Brody's house and laughs "hey baby" I shake my head and walk towards her "come on sleepy head" I wrap my arm around hers and head back into the house and stick her back into bed "now stay" I shake my head and walk towards my room and shake my head before running downstairs and into the kitchen. I grab a bottle of water from the fridge and look out the back yard shaking my head "what are we going to do with her" I smirk and turn around and walk toward the kitchen door. I turn the light out and jump when I hear a bang coming from outside and quickly turn around and see someone outside wearing black clothing and a balaclava crawling along the grass 'surely she hasn't jumped out the window?' I grab my phone from my pocket but it dies as I unlock it 'typical' I look around and see a flashlight hanging up and smile "that will do" I grab it and run out the kitchen and towards my bedroom "please work" I open my curtains and turn the flashlight on shinning it into Brody's room and after a few seconds I see him appear at the window opening it looking pissed of "what?!" I shake my head and place my finger towards my mouth "shh!" I point towards the back yard and Brody's eye shoot awake "stay there!" He grabs something before closing his window and disappearing out the room. I shake my head and take a deep breath "dammit Brody" I look towards the back yard and see the figure looking towards me before quickly running towards the kitchen door "oh no this can't be good" I run towards Roxy's room and slam the door waking her "what?!" She jumps up and I shake my head and grab her arm "shh" I walk towards the other side of her bed and shake my head "hide" she kneels down and hides under the bed and I look around and spot a signed hockey stick and grab it before heading towards the back of the door. I look towards the bed and see Roxy hiding under it shaking her head towards me so I close my eyes and take a deep breath and lock my eyes onto the door handle and after a few seconds it moves and the door starts to open so I hold the hockey stick tighter before swinging it towards the door and hitting someone knocking them to the ground. I look towards Roxy as she hides her head in her head and looks towards the ground "did you get them?" I look behind the door and see a body lying on the ground "yeah." I walk towards the body and shake my head "it's Brody" Roxy runs towards me and shakes her head "what?" I bend down and shake my head "Brody?" Roxy laughs nervously and steps over him "I'll get the ice" she runs downstairs and I take a deep breath and stroke his face "Brody?" He moves his hand onto my knee and I smile and stroke his face "hey!" He opens his eyes and smiles "hi" he licks his lip before sitting up "take it easy I think I might have hurt you" he rubs his head and smiles "I'm fine" he stands up and holds his hands out "come on" I take his hands and smile "are you sure?" He nods and smirks "yes" he moves a little closer to me and locks his eyes onto my lips. Roxy runs upstairs holding a bag of ice "here you go" Brody looks at the ice and shakes his head "I'm fine" he smiles at me and shrugs "I should go" he walks downstairs and Roxy looks at me and shrugs "what was that about?" I shrug and sigh "I don't know" I shake my head and smile "but I'm going to find out" I run down the stairs after Brody and he stops at the kitchen door and smiles "that person ran away before I could get him" I look around the back garden and smile "thank you for coming over" he nods firmly and smirks "anytime" he rubs his head and laughs nervously "just no more sticks please" I look down and laugh softly "noted" I look at him and see his huge green eyes looking right at me and it made my whole body shiver and my palms sweat "goodnight Brody" he nods and smiles "goodnight Amy, sweet dreams" he leaves and closes the back door behind him so I walk towards it and lock it before running towards the kitchen window and watch him walk into his house before taking a deep breath "this motto is not working for me anymore." I head towards the living room and let Bear out and take a deep breath "come on boy" I head back upstairs and he follows me into my bedroom and tries to jump up onto my bed "nice try." I walk over towards his bed and smile "come on buddy" he runs over towards me and lies down and drifts of to sleep instantly "night buddy" I stand up and see Brody's room light turn on so I walk towards my window swimming and see him pacing up and down his room on the phone so I shake my head and smile "night Brody!" I wave and he looks over and smiles before waving and closing his curtains "ok then!" I shake my head and close my window and curtains before heading into bed and falling straight too sleep.

I wake up the next morning when Roxy runs into my room laughing shaking me "get up!" I quickly sit up and shake my head "what?" I look around and look at my alarm clock "it's 7AM what do you want?" She rolls her eyes and sits down on my bed holding her phone "look" she shows me her phone and I rub my eyes and look at the screen and see a news article "Bar attack?" I look at her and raise my eyebrows "look at the names" she rolls her eyes and I look at it and smile "Nathan Smith" she nods and laughs sarcastically "that's Karma that is" I laugh softly and shake my head "when was this?" She sits up and looks at it "last night" her face drops and she shakes her head and falls back into the bed "it was in Jackson" I look at her phone and shake my head "that's" she looks at me and nods "only 500 miles away" I stand up and pace the room "that doesn't mean that he's coming here though" I shrug and look at her "he can't know where we are" she looks at me and shrugs "we was careful" I nod and sit down next to her "I'm sure he doesn't so let's try not worry about it and we will be fine if we keep to the plan" she stands up and nods "your right" she looks towards under my bed and nods "you done it?" I nod and look down "yes" she smiles and takes a deep breath "good" she walks towards the room door and stops and looks at Bear "you want breakfast boy?" Bear sits up and runs by her side "let's go" she heads towards the door shaking her head "I'm going to start breakfast" I stand up and nod "I will get ready for school and be down" she turns around and nods towards the window "it's a nice day so I can give you one of my dresses?" She smirks and I roll my eyes shaking my head "I will use my own thank you" she shrugs and walks away "breakfast will be ready in 10" I look under my bed and take a deep breath "ok." I grab a dress from my drawers and start getting ready for school before running downstairs and join Roxy in the kitchen "here" she hands me a plate of toast and scrambled egg and a glass of orange juice "thank you" I sit down and eat into my toast "we should really send that James boy a bunch of flowers or something" I laugh softly nearly choking on my toast "what?" She sits down next to me and smirks "that's twice he has come here and been attacked" she eats into her toast and I smirk and shake my head "came here to try help us too" she laughs nervously and shrugs "well you can apologise for me when you see him at school" I smile and nod "I will." I finish my toast and stand up "can you drop me of at school?" She looks at the clock and nods "yeah" she stands up and sticks the plates in the sink "go get your bag and shoes and we can leave" I walk into the hallway and grab my shoes and grab my bag from the back of the cupboard door "let's go" Roxy hands Bear a slice of toast and strokes his head "be a good boy" she walks out the kitchen and follows me towards her car. The drive to school is quite and all I can think about is Brody and how he told me to stay away from him but he keeps helping me. He could have got seriously hurt last night but he still risked it, why? I was determined to get answers from him. When we pull up Roxy hands me a key and money "I will be late coming home tonight so order yourself pizza or something and keep me a few slices" I smile and nod "ok" I take the key and money and stick them in my bag "have fun" she laughs softly and waves "you too." I walk towards the school doors looking at the ground thinking about what I'm going to say too Brody 'will he even speak to me?' I shake my head and look up and see Ryder standing at the top of the stairs smirking "good morning" I smile and wave "hey" he raises his eyebrows in confusion and shakes his head "not a good morning?" I laugh nervously and look down "sorry I'm just tired" he goes into his bag and grabs a can of energy juice and hands me it "here" I look at the can and shake my head "thank you" I take a sip of the can leaving my peach pink lipstick around it "can I?" Ryder holds his hand out and I smile and hand him the can and he takes a sip without cleaning the can leaving a bit of my lipstick on his face "thanks" he hands me it back and I shake my head and laugh nervously "you got a little" I point towards his mouth and he smile and shrugs "what?" I shake my head and look down laughing nervously. "Amy?" I turn around and smile when I hear Brody's voice but he was the opposite from smiling, he looks at Ryder and see's my lipstick and looks at the ground shaking his head "never mind" he runs upstairs and hands Ryder a napkin "you got lipstick on your face" he look at me disappointed "it's not your colour Ryder" I take a deep breath and open my mouth to explain myself but he walks inside without saying another word. I shake my head and smile towards Ryder "sorry" I run after Brody but he disappears into the boy's bathroom "Brody wait!" I shake my head and look down "it's not what it looked like" I take a deep breath and look up 'let's just get this day over with.' I walk down the hallway and spot Noah running into the cafeteria so I smile and nod 'I'm sure he will talk some sense into

Brody' I run after him and see him run out towards the football field so I run after him and go out the exit door and look around for him 'bingo!' I smile as I spot him speaking to someone, I walk towards him not acknowledging my surroundings so I don't turn around until after I hear someone shout my name. As I turn around I look up and see it flying towards me, to close for me to move and it hits me in the face knocking me onto the ground making me go unconscious.

I feel myself coming back around so I open my eyes to see a bright light above me. I finally see clearly and realise I am in a nurse office 'what?' I look around and sit up rubbing my head 'ouch' I see an ice pack next to me so I grab it and place it on my bruised head and swing my legs around the bed and jump of it. I spot my bag on a chair by the door so I walk towards it and get my phone and check the time '9:15' I smile and nod 'I've only missed 15 minutes of class' I open the door and see a nurse standing outside filling out a form "Miss Thomas?" I nod and walk towards her "yeah that's me" she looks back at the form in front of her and looks towards my head "may

I see your head?" I nod and move the ice pack and let her see the bruise "I'm going to write you a note to leave and go home" I shake my head and move the ice pack "no please" she looks at me and smiles "I'm fine." She looks at my head and sighs "fine" she writes on two pieces of paper's and hands me them "this one is for your teacher to explain why are you are late" she hands me the other and smiles "and this is if you feel dizzy or anything then give this to a teacher and you will be able to go home" I nod and take the paper "I will" I smile and hand her the ice pack "thank you" I walk towards the exit before she can change her mind or say another word and quickly walk down the hallway and towards Maths class. I open the maths classroom door and everyone including Mr Blackwood looks at me "Amy?" Mr Blackwood stands up and looks towards Ricky sitting at the back of the classroom with his head down "I thought you went home?" I shake my head and hand him my note from the nurse "no" I smile softly and shrug "I'm fine" he places the note on his desk without even looking and nods "ok" he points towards the back of the class and smiles "take a seat then and enjoy the movie" I look towards the screen behind Mr Blackwood and see another film on. I walk towards the back of the classroom and sit in the chair next to Ricky "are you ok?" I nod and smile "yeah I'm fine" he takes a deep breath and leans towards me "I am so so sorry" I laugh softly and shake my head "you flung the ball?" He leans back on his chair and nods "yeah" I smile and lean back on mine shaking my head "it's fine" I look towards the movie and rub my head "I'm fine." Once the bell rings Ricky stands up and rushes out the room like he was trying to avoid me but I shake my head and take a deep breath and walk out after him. I walk down the hallway and stop at the top of the stairs when I hear a crowd of people at the bottom of the stairs chanting "fight fight fight fight" I smile and try get a better look 'I could witness my first high school fight here' the crowd move and I get a look at the two people in the middle and see Brody taking his jacket of "oh no!" I run down the stairs and push past and get too the front and see Ricky taking his bag of and getting ready to fight. Brody smirks and steps forward flinging the first punch making Ricky's nosebleed "hey!" I step in front of them and shake my head "enough!" Brody looks at me like he has just jaw a ghost "Amy?!" I raise my eyebrows and nod "last time I checked?" he shakes his head and looks towards Noah "but I thought you was in hospital with a broken nose and 2 black eyes?" I look at Noah and he steps back through the crowd and I shake my head "what?" I look at Ricky and laugh nervously "no!" I look back at Brody and point towards my head "I got a bruised head but other than that I'm fine" he grabs his jacket from the floor and shakes his head towards Ricky "stay out my way Stone!" He pushes past the crowd of people and follows the direction Noah went into. I look at Ricky and smile "you ok?" He smiles and nods "yeah I'm fine" I grab his bag from the ground and hand him it "come on" I wrap my arm around his and walk down the hallway towards English. We get to the top of the stairs and I hear an angry voice from behind "Mr Stone my office now!" Ricky sighs and turns around "I will see you later Amy" he removes his arm from around mine and I smile "ok." The woman looks at me and shakes her head "you too Miss Thomas" she nods and turns around storming her feet down the hallway "who is that?" I look at Ricky and he laughs nervously and wraps his arm around mine "that is our head teacher" I take a deep breath and walk with Ricky down the stairs and down the hallway after her. She holds her office door open and I walk in after Ricky and sit down next to him "so you want to explain what happened?" She sits down and looks at Ricky "it was all a misunderstanding" I sit forward and shake my head "I heard about what happened with the football" she looks at Ricky and smirks "does it have anything to do with that?" She looks at me and leans back on her chair "because I do not tolerate violence in this school Miss Thomas" I nod and look down "I know I would never" I take a deep breath and look up "like I said Miss it was all a misunderstanding" she looks at Ricky and nods "ok" she stands up and points towards the door "just stay out of trouble Mr Stone and watch where you fling your ball" Ricky giggles before standing up "yes Miss June" he nods and walks towards the door and I follow after him "close the door please Miss Thomas" I look behind and close the door as I exit and follow Ricky out into the hallway. I spot Noah and Brody at Brody's locker speaking before looking over towards us, Brody steps forward and Noah grabs his arm and shakes his head "not worth it." Ricky takes a deep breath and looks at the ground "I should go" he runs of down the hallway before I could stop him "Ricky wait!" I look at him as he runs down the hallway and upstairs. I look towards Brody as he slams his locker "what?!" I shake my head and take a deep breath before walking towards the reception and handing the man behind the desk my note from the nurse and running out the exit doors. As I run outside I feel the cold rain hit me running down my legs 'I knew I should have brought a jacket' I run down the street towards my house in the pouring rain 'this is why I use the motto no boys.' When I get to the house I open the door and slam it behind me and run upstairs leaving wet dirty footprints on the stairs carpet and run into my bedroom slamming the door behind me and diving onto my bed with my face into my pillow and screaming into it. I take a deep breath and stand up "ok now that's over with" I hear barking and smile "Bear?" I hear scratching at my door so I run towards it and open it and see Bear sitting at the other side of my door wagging his tail "hey boy" he runs in and sits by my bed "fine" I walk towards him and lift him onto my bed "just while I have a shower" I stroke his head and smile. I take a deep breath and look around my room "I should get out these clothes first" I walk towards my drawers and grab clean clothes and get my dressing gown from the back of my door and place my clothes on the chair and head into my bathroom placing my dressing gown on the hook by the shower and turn the shower on and leave it to warm up. I look into the mirror and run my hands along my hair "I can't stand rain" I take a deep breath and head into the shower letting the water run down my back I drift off into my own thoughts about Brody and him kicking off with Ricky, I didn't want that around me and I didn't want some BOY thinking he has to come to my rescue. I was angry and I was going to make sure it didn't happen again. The front doorbell rings and I jump and turn the shower of "who can that be?" I shake my head and grab my bath robe and slippers and run out the bathroom and see Bear jump of the bed and out the room, I run after him downstairs and towards the front door opening it. "Hello?" I take a deep breath and step back inside and close the door looking at Bear "weird" I run back upstairs and grab my clothes and get changed and get one of my books from my bedside drawer and sit in the middle of my bed with my legs crossed about to start reading my book but stop when I see Bear running in my room "come on then" I lean over the edge and pick him up and he lies at the bottom of my bed and falls asleep "your cute sometimes" I smile and start reading the first few chapters but stop when I hear screaming coming from outside 'what is going on out there?' I stand up and walk towards my window looking out and see Brody's window open. I look towards Brody's room and see him and that same girl from before sitting on his bed. Brody spots me and stops laughing and stands up and walks towards his window and smirks before closing it 'weirdo!' I scoff and shut my window and close my curtains 'who does he think he is?' I take a deep breath and walk back towards my bed and sit down before reading the rest of the book. I drift off into my book trying to block out Brody that I don't notice my bedroom door open or see Ryder standing by the door smirking at me "hey" I smile and look back towards my book not engaging "Ryder?!" I stick my book down making Bear jump "how did you get in here?" He smirks and walks in "your cousin let me in." He holds a bag up and shrugs "I brought sweets" I roll my eyes and smile "what did you bring?" He hands me a bar of chocolate and smiles "what's the catch?" He sits down and shrugs "I heard about today so thought you could use some cheering up" I smile and take the chocolate "thank you." He smiles and nods "your welcome." Bear stretches and walks towards Ryder and licks his hand "friend for life" Ryder smirks and nods "good." He stands up and walks towards the window opening the curtains and window laughing sarcastically "It's like 100 degrees in here why you not have this open?" He takes a sniff of the fresh air and looks out the window laughing softly "oh look Jennifer's in town" I stand up and roll my eyes 'great Jennifer must be the girl in Brody's room' I walk towards the window and smile "Jennifer another one of yours and Brody's ex's?" I reach the window and see the girl sitting on Brody's bed "what?" Ryder looks at me and shakes his head laughing nervously "no she's Brody's cousin" he waves and she eventually looks over smiling and waving "hey you!" She opens the window and leans forward "hey Ryder!" She looks behind her and I spot Brody walking in the door smiling "who you speaking too?" Brody walks towards the window and Jennifer looks back over towards us "Ryder" he rushes towards the window and looks at me "what you doing there?" he looks at Ryder and fakes smiles "just over cheering Amy up" I smirk and nod "chocolate always cheers a girl up" I smirk and close the window "got to go" I smirk towards Brody as I turn around "now let's eat this chocolate" I walk back towards the bed and sit down "you want some?" Ryder walks towards me and sits down "yeah why not" my bedroom door opens and Roxy walks in holding a tray with two cups and a bar of chocolate and marshmallows "hey kids" she looks at me and smirks "here youse go" she sticks it on my bedside table and looks at Bear and nods "let's go for a walk and leave these two to study" she walks out the bedroom with Bear running behind her. I shake my head and laugh nervously "study?" Ryder smirks and shrugs "I had to tell her something" I roll my eyes and grab a book from my bag "guess we could study?" Ryder smirks and leans back "I didn't bring any books" I roll my eyes and scoff "so what did you bring?" He lifts his bag up and smirks "movies and sweets" he stands up and walks towards my TV "what kind of movie do you like?" I get comfortable and smile "something scary" he nods and smirks "I like you're thinking" he sticks a movie in and empty's his bag onto the bed and crisp's and sweets fall onto it "now move over" he takes his shoes and jacket of and lays next to me "good studying this" he looks at me and smiles "I know right?" He turns back towards the TV and I shake my head and start to watch the movie. After half an hour I grab a bag of Crisp's and open them "thanks" Ryder grabs a handful and I scoff and shake my head "welcome" I eat some and stick them in between us "that hot chocolate will be cold" I look over towards the tray and smile "I forgot about that" he reaches over and hands me a cup spilling it over my jumper "sorry" I take the cup and shake my head "It's fine" I stick the cup onto the table next to me and smile "I have a t-shirt on under it" I take my jumper of but it takes my top with it and gets stuck halfway of "my t-shirt is coming of too isn't it?" Ryder laughs softly "yeah." He reaches for the remote and presses pause "let me help you" I feel him touch the top of my arm and he pulls the jumper of making my t-shirt come off with its "thanks" I turn my t-shirt inside out and jump dropping it when my bedroom door swings open "well doesn't this look nice." I look over and see Brody standing smirking with his arms crossed "what do you want James?" Ryder rolls his eyes and walks in the room towards us "not coming to see you anyway."

He looks at me and smiles "I am here to see her" I stick my t-shirt back on and roll my eyes "why?" He shrugs and smiles "why not?" He looks towards the TV and laughs softly "I love this movie" he takes his shoes of and sits in the middle of us and watches the TV "play it then" I take a deep breath and shake my head grabbing the remote and pressing play. I look towards Ryder and mouth 'sorry' she smiles and shakes his head mouthing 'it's fine' I laugh softly and face the TV and watch the rest of the movie. 'This is not what I had in mind when I said no boys' I look at Brody and Ryder and shake my head and face the TV again 'I need air.' Once the movie finishes I sigh in relief and stand up and quickly walk towards my drawers and grab my camera "youse can let yourselves out" I smirk and run out the room leaving Ryder and Brody still lying on my bed "Amy wait!" I downstairs before they even get up from the bed and grab my shoes from the bottom of the stairs and sticking them on and running out the front door closing it behind me. 'I thought that movie was never going to end' I run out the gate and down the street looking towards my camera 'why is this setting black and white?' I click through my pictures and see photos of Bear 'Roxy!' I roll my eyes and change the settings still walking down the street not watching were I'm walking and not seeing someone walking towards me on their phone. I hit into them dropping my camera out my hand "no!" I see two hands catch my camera and laugh "we need to stop meeting like this" I look up and see the boy from before standing in front of me smirking holding my camera out "hi" I look into his sparkly green eyes and blush "hello." He smirks and I take the camera from him and wrap it around my neck "I don't mind" I smirk and shrug "as long as you keep catching my camera" he smiles and nods "deal." He shakes his head and laughs softly "you heading back into the woods?" I smile and nod "yeah" she turns around and face's the way I'm walking and smirks "good" he wraps his arm around mine and walks down the street "I need to find Bella." I laugh nervously and walk down the street with him "who's Bella?" He looks at me and winks "girlfriend?" I look down a smile nervously "no" I look at him and see him smirking "she's my dog" I laugh in relief and he shrugs "well my sisters' dog." We turn into the woods and he takes a deep breath "I kind of lost her and need help to find her if you fancy it?" I nod firmly and smile "of course! I would be sad if I lost my dog" he nods and squeezes my arm softly "thank you." We walk deeper into the woods he calls for Bella's name and I join in not taking my eyes of him until he looks towards me, after the third time he laughs nervously and shakes his head "what?" I shake my head and look down "nothing" he smirks and shakes his head "I never did catch your name" he looks at me and smiles "Amy" he nods and kisses my hand "Liam" I blush and look down "now let's find your sisters dog." We walk around for the next half hour speaking about anything and everything and he stops and looks around "did you hear that?" I stop and listen and hear barking "yeah" He runs up the hill "this way" I take a deep breath and run up the hill after him and he stops at the top of the hill and smiles "there she is!" I look down the hill where he is pointing and spot a little black "good" I run down the hill and laugh "race you" Liam laughs softly and runs after me. I reach the dog first and he shakes his head "I win!" Liam laughs nervously and tickles me "you cheated" I roll my eyes and smirk "bad loser?" He bends down and stokes the dog "hey girl" I look at the small pup in front of me and shake my head "she looks like" I look around and shake my head "what?" I laugh nervously and shrug "nothing" he raises his eyebrows and smiles "you sure?" Liam picks the dog up and I keep looking at it closely "it's just" I move closer and smile "it looks exactly like my dog bear" I stroke the dogs head and it sniffs my hand and licks it "about the same age to." I shake my head and stand back "I found Bear in these woods" I look at him and nod "that day I bumped into you" he smirks and shrugs "literally." I laugh softly and nod "come on and I will see if my cousin has brought him back yet" he picks Bella up and we walk back out the woods. As we walk back through the woods and I can't help but feel like Roxy is going to give me an earful tonight about bringing three boys to the house in the one day so I look at Liam and smile " doesn't take well to strangers but if you wait outside I will bring him out and we can go a double doggy walk?" Liam looks at me and smiles sending butterfly's through my stomach "ok." We get out the woods and back onto the sidewalk and I nod towards my house "this way" he follows me down the street still holding Bella in his arms like she was a little baby. I stop and look towards my house when we reach it and laugh nervously "I won't be long" I look towards Brody's house and take a deep breath 'I hope they have left' I open the gate and walk in "you live here?" I look at Liam and nod "yeah why?" He looks at Brody's house and smiles "I know it's the old spy's house but it's really nice" he looks back towards me and smiles "yeah that's it" he nods and I laugh nervously and turn around and run towards the house opening the door and closing it behind me. I take a deep breath and look into the living room "hello?" I walk into the kitchen and see Bear sleeping in his bed "hey boy" he wakes up and runs towards my wagging his tail "where's Roxy?" I stand up and walk towards the stairs "Roxy!" After a few seconds I take a deep breath and open the front door and look towards Liam and smile "come on" he looks at me and points towards himself "me?" I laugh softly and nod "yes you" he comes in my gate and closes it behind him letting Bella down on the floor and walking towards me "what about your cousin?" I open my door wide and smile "she isn't in" Bear runs towards the door and barks towards Liam and he looks down and laughs sarcastically "hello little guy" he bends down and Bear licks his hand "he is like Bella" Bella runs over towards us and pounces on Bear and licks his face "you don't think that?" I look at Liam and shrug "I don't know" I look behind Liam and see Brody coming out his house and I laugh nervously and pull Liam in "let's find out" Brody looks over and spots Liam and opens his mouth to speak but I slam the door shut before he can get the chance. I turn around and face Liam "let's go upstairs" he smiles and I shake my head 'Brody can see right into my bedroom' I walk towards the living room and shake my head "this will be fine" I look towards the dogs and shrug "don't want dog poo on my floor" he nods and follows me into the living room and sits down "drink?" He nods and smiles "cola ok?" I quickly walk into the kitchen without knowing his reply and look out the kitchen window and see Brody hanging out his room window looking towards my room "I think people got the spy's in the wrong address!" I turn around and see Liam walking towards me "what?" I laugh nervously and shake my head "oh just me speaking to myself" he smirks and nods "are you ok?" I walk towards the fridge and grab two cans of cola 'no' I hand him one and smile "yeah why?" He takes the can and smiles "you just seem a little weird" I laugh nervously and look down 'act normal Amy' I shake my head and take a deep breath "sorry" he smirks and looks down "it's fine" he looks at me and shrugs "I think it's kinda cute actually." I look at him and blush smirking from cheek to cheek "really?" He nods and leans forward locking his eyes onto my lips but stops and sighs "maybe next time" he steps back and I shake my head "what?" I blush and breath through my nose 'does my breath smell?' He smirks and looks towards the kitchen window and I follow his eyes and see Brody standing outside "Brody!" I stick my can of cola down and shake my head "sorry about him" I walk towards the back door and open it "what are you doing here?" He looks past me and into my kitchen towards Liam "what are you doing here?" I raise my eyebrows and laugh nervously "ehh I live here?" He looks at me and laughs shaking his head "not you" he leans back folding his arms and looking at Liam "him!" I look at Liam and smile "youse know each other?" Liam walks towards us and scoffs "Liam is my cousin" I nearly choke with laughter that I send tears coming out my eyes "wait what?" I look at Liam and wipe my eyes "really?" I look at Bella as she walks into the kitchen and nod "and I take it Jennifer is your sister?" Liam looks at me and raises his eyebrow "you know my sister?" Brody smirks and looks me up and down "she thought she was my girlfriend and got all jealous" I roll my eyes at Brody and start closing the back door "I did not now bye Brody" I close it and lock it behind me and look at Liam "thanks for the heads up." Liam shakes his head and walks towards the window and closes the curtains "I didn't know you stayed here or I would have" I smile and take a deep breath "it doesn't matter if he is" I look towards Bear and Bella and nod "we are here to find out if these dogs come from the same litter" he smirks and walks towards the kitchen door and nods "come on" he walks out the kitchen and into the living room "so where did you get Bella?" I follow him into the living room and sit on the sofa across from him and he sits Bella on his lap and smiles "Jeremy got Jennifer her two weeks ago when her fish died and said he will keep it here for her" I look out the window towards Jeremys house and smile "did he say where he got her from?" I look at him and he shrugs "no but it's not really something you ask" she looks at Bear as he runs into the living room "so you found Bear? Did you not think you should take him to the vets for a check-up?" I lift him up on the sofa beside me and shake my head "no he looked healthy to me and I just thought that he was from a stray litter and escaped I guess" I look at Liam and he shakes his head and stands up "let's go" I raise my eyebrows and smirk "where?" He looks at

Bear and lifts Bella "vets for a check-up" I look at Bear and nod "fine but I think you should get Bella one because they look like they are from the same litter" he looks towards Bella and smiles "deal" he looks at me and nods "let's go." He walks out the room and I grab Bear and follow him out "who are you?" I hear Roxy's voice from outside "Liam" I laugh softly and pop my head out "he's with me" she looks Liam up and down and nods "nice" she shakes her head and smiles "where are youse going?" She looks towards Bear and I smile "vets" she looks towards Bella in Liam's arms and shakes her head "there is now two Bear's?" I smile and shake my head "no this is Bella" I looks at Bear and smirk "we think they are from the same litter though." Roxy nods firmly and smiles "I see" she looks behind her and shrugs "youse want a ride?" Liam looks at me and nods "the vets is about 3 miles away so that would be great" I nod and smile "thank you." Liam walks towards the car and Roxy smirks towards me "don't" she shrugs and walks towards the car beside me "what?" I roll my eyes and shove her gently "just don't" she laughs softly and looks towards the floor "love the number three" I open the car door and roll my eyes "just drive" she gets in and laughs "buckle up kiddo's." I stick my belt on and smile at Liam "thanks for coming with me" he smiles and places his hand on my knee "of course" I blush and smile as his warm firm hand touches me 'what is he doing too me?' I look at Roxy and see her looking at us through the rear-view mirror smirking 'I don't know what I like it.' I look at Liam and smile "what?" I shake my head and look down towards Bear "nothing" he moves his hand up my leg and touches my hand and squeezes it "so are you guys like dating?" I look at Roxy and raise my eyebrows "what?" She looks into the rear-view mirror and smiles "just asking" she smirks and shrugs before looking back towards the road 'I didn't know what this was or why he was so sweet towards me but we definitely was NOT dating' I look at Liam and smile 'even if he was really beautiful' he smiles towards me and I look towards Bear trying to hide the fact I was blushing 'I don't do boys and I definitely do not date." We eventually pull up outside the vets and Liam moves his hand and opens his door and gets out still holding Bella in her hand before closing it behind it "I want details" I look at Roxy and shake my head "there isn't any details" she raises her eyebrows and I go too open my door but see Liam open it for me "my lady" I laugh nervously and shake my head "thank you." I get out the car and close the door "hey!" I look at Roxy and she smirks rolling her window down "so pizza and catch up later?" I roll my eyes and nod "fine" she looks towards Liam and nods "look after her" he walks towards me and holds my hand "I will" my stomach does cartwheels and I smile and blush as his warm strong hand falls perfectly into place with mine 'I could get use to this' I smile and wave "bye Roxy" I walk towards the vets with Bear in one hand and Liam in the other following behind me. I push the door open and look at Bear as he barks and licks my hand "don't be scared buddy" he sticks his head into me and I smile "you will be fine." Liam let's go of my hand and points towards a cabinet with leaflets and smiles "I will be over in a minute" I nod and smile "ok"

I walk towards the reception and a woman looks up from the desk and looks at me "how can I help you?" I smile and nod towards Bear "just for a check-up" she looks at her computer and starts typing "dogs name" I look at bear and smile "bear" she looks at him and smirks "date of birth" I laugh nervously and shake my head "I don't know" she looks at me and raises her eyebrow "he's a stray that I found" she gives me a fake smile and nods "have a seat please" I smile nervously and nod "thank you" I walk over towards the empty seats and sit down looking at Bear "there's a good boy." I look up and see Liam walking towards me holding a handful of leaflets "here" he hands me them and smiles "got you a few puppy information leaflets" I smile and place them on the empty seat next to me "thank you." The reception looks up and smiles "can I help you?" Liam looks over and shakes his head "just here supporting my" he looks at me and shrugs "girlfriend" I nearly choke and laugh nervously 'did he just call me his girlfriend? And since when did I agree to that?' I look down and blush 'I'm sure he was joking' I look at him and laugh 'right?'

The reception woman looks towards Bella and nods "that dog looks like bear" I look at her and smile "we think she might be from the same litter" she nods towards Liam "bring it over" Liam stands up and walks towards the reception and she suddenly starts playing with her hair and bats her eyelashes at him "do you want me to get a vet to check?" Liam laughs sarcastically "if my girlfriend wants" he looks at me and I laugh embarrassed "yeah why not" she looks at me and gives me another fake smile before looking me up and down "ok I will get the vet to see them both" Liam smiles and nods "thank you" he walks back towards me and sits down "she wants me" I laugh nervously and shake my head "I can tell." He holds my hand and smirks "you jealous?" I roll my eyes and scoff "you wish" I look down and shake my head "and when was I your girlfriend?" He smirks at me showing me his amazing teeth and gives me these big puppy dog eyes with his amazing green sparkly eyes "I just didn't want her flirting with me" I roll my eyes and smile "must be so hard that" he shakes his head and looks down "it is." An older man with amazing shiny slick back hair and large brown eyes walk out with a clipboard and smiles towards us "Bear?" I smile and stand up "that's us" he nods towards the room he came from and smiles "this way please" he walks into the room and I smile at Liam and nod "ready?" He smiles and nods "yeah" I walk into the room with Liam following behind me and he closes the door after him. "How can I help?" I look towards Bear and smile "just for a check-up" he looks at Bear and smiles "strange breed of dog" he taps the table and I place Bear on it and he examines him "what kind of dog is he?" He looks at me and smirks "youse bought a dog without knowing the breed?" I laugh nervously and look at Bear "I didn't buy him" I look at the veterinary and shrug "I found him" the veterinary quickly backs away and grabs a black box from his shelf and sits it on the table "he's a Norwegian Lundehund." He looks at Bella and smiles "they both are" I look at Liam and smile "are they from the same breed?" The vet grabs a stethoscope and places it on Bear's back "hmm" I shake my head and lean forward "what?" He nods towards Liam and smiles "bring that one." Liam walks over and place's Bella on the table and he examines her "they are both healthy" he sticks the black box back and smiles "they are about 4 months old and from the same litter of Norwegian Lundehund's are not very common never mind in a small town like this." He clicks on his laptop and prints of sheets of papers "give this is Susan and she will register the dogs and make youse a new appointment in 6 months to see how they are doing" I take the paper's and hand Liam one "thank you" he nods and sits down "bye" I pick up Bear and walk out the room with Liam following behind me. I look at the woman in reception and she smiles "yes?" I hand her the piece of paper and she smiles "I will just need a few details from youse" I smile and nod "ok" she hands us 2 forms and clipboards and we sit down too fill them in. 'Name' I look at Liam and see him concentrating filling his form out, I look at his face and smile when I see his tounge hanging out his mouth 'name? Amy.' I fill the rest of the form in and Liam holds his hand out "thank you" he walks towards reception and hands them to the woman and walks back towards me smiling "ready?" I stand up and pick up Bear "yeah." I follow him out the vets and I grab my phone from my pocket and look around "shall I call Roxy?" Liam shakes his head and smiles "I want to show you something first" he hands me Bears lead and I stick it on him and let him down "come on it's not far" he starts walking down the street and I follow him until he stops a few feet down the street "we are here" I look to the side of the pavement and see a forest park "good job you wore comfy shoes" I raise my eyebrows and laugh nervously "where are we going?" He smirks and nods "you will see" I follow him into the gate and he closes it behind us and we walk deep into the forest. 'Where is he taking me?' I look down as we continue to walk deeper into the forest and he eventually stops and smirks "what?" He steps back and grins and I start feeling weird, my stomach goes tense and I look around 'what's going on? Why did he really bring me here?' I clench my fist and step back 'is this a trap?' He smiles and holds his hand out clenched up "look" I look at his hand and he turns it around and opens it "what?" After a few seconds of awkward silence he looks up and I follow his eyes and see the stars start to appear one by one above us "wow" I smirk and look up that long my neck hurts "this place is amazing" he smirks and nods towards the top of the hill "it's better the higher you go but I didn't want you to miss it" I smile and look up "they are so pretty" he smirks and looks at me "maybe one day we can go higher and see it?" I smile and nod "I would love that" he nods and laughs softly "good now let's get you back before your cousin has my head for thanksgiving dinner" I smile and follow him back out towards the forest. He opens the gate and closes it behind us "why do you close it?" He nods towards the road and smiles "in case a deer gets out and causes damage" he nods towards a sign by the gate "please keep gate locked at all times" I nod and smile "that makes sense." I follow him back up the street and he grabs his phone as it dings "your ride is here" I raise my eyebrow and shake my head "what?" A car pulls up next to us and I see Jeremy in the driver side smiling "get in loser" I smile nervously at

Liam and he laughs nervously "you didn't think I was going to let you walk back did you?" He smiles and hugs me "night" I smile softly and hug him back "goodnight" he opens the back door and I get in holding Bear in my arms "see you tomorrow?" I nod and smile "ok" he closes the door and waves "don't crash Jeremy" Jeremy looks at me through the rear-view mirror and smirks "I will try my best" he speeds of before Liam can say another word and I quickly stick my seat belt on and hold onto it. 'Please don't answer any awkward questions' I smile at him as he still continues to look at me through the rear-view mirror 'just don't make eye contact' I look out the window for a few seconds and look back and see him still look towards me. "What?" Still looking at me like I stole the last chocolate biscuit he shrugs and smiles "nothing" I roll my eyes and look back out the window. He stops outside his house and quickly undo's his belt "I know what you're doing" I grab my door and shake my head "I'm not doing anything?" He smirks and locks the doors "what the hell Jeremy?!" I try open the door and shake my head "let me out" he smirks and leans back "I will" he looks me up and down "if you stay away from my brother and cousin" he looks towards his house and I shake my head "what? No they are my friends" he shrugs and leans back "then I guess it's going to be a long night" I shake my head and try open the door harder "Jeremy let me out!" He rolls his eyes and smirks "you're so dramatic" he clicks lock button and the doors unlock making me open my side door and fall out the car onto the cold wet grass. "What the hell Jeremy?" I quickly stand up and he gets out the car and smirks "just stay away from them or I will make your life here hell" he looks towards my house and shrugs "you will wish you came back from wherever you came from" he leans forward and his voice sounds serious and angry like I was his worst enemy 'what was his problem?' He looks at me and leans forward "that's a good girl" I smirk and shake my head "fuck you" I slap his face making a red Craig but he grabs it before I can move it back and smirks "this is going to be fun" he squeezes my hand making it burn, a pain like no other "ouch Jeremy you are hurting me" he scoffs and looks me up and down "just do what I say and we won't have a problem" he lets me go and stands up straight smiling. "Hey Brody" I look over towards his door and see Brody standing in his shorts topless "what's going on?" I look at Jeremy and he smirks and raises his eyebrow "nothing" I shake my head and mouth 'you're a monster' I pick up Bear and turn around climbing the fence and run into the house slamming the door behind me. "Amy?" I stick Bear down and smile trying to hold my tears in "yeah it's me" Roxy pops her head out from the kitchen and holds a pizza box up "gossip time?" I give her a fake smile and shake my head "tomorrow?" I yawn and fake laugh "I'm going bed" I run upstairs before she tries to change my mind and run towards me bed and stick my head into the pillow filling it with my tears. 'What the hell is Jeremys problem and why does he want me to stay away from Brody and Liam so badly for?' I sit up and wipe my tears 'wonder if Brody knows anything about it.' I stand up and walk towards my window and see Brody's room light on "Brody?" I see a shadow appear to the window and close the curtains 'ok then' I take a deep breath and close the window and curtains and head into the bathroom and wash my face. I look into the mirror and smile 'jerks' I head into the bedroom and get changed into my pjs and get into bed closing my eyes and drift of straight away.

The next morning I wake up and roll over onto my back 'I really don't want to move' I look at my alarm clock and shake my head 'but I have school in an hour' I get up and stick on clothes and head downstairs where Roxy is already cooked breakfast "morning" I smile and sit down "morning" she hands me a glass of orange juice and smirks "so?" I shrug and take a sip "what?" She hands me a plate of toast and bacon "what's the goss?" I shrug and eat a slice of toast "there isn't any" I smile and shrug "none?" I nod firmly and laugh nervously "sorry" she takes a deep breath and shakes her head "I thought he was going to make a move" I smile and look at my toast "nope." She grabs her car keys and jacket and smiles "you ready?" I grab my toast and eat another slice before giving the rest of Bear "yeah" I follow her out towards the car and get in without looking at Brody's house. Roxy gets in and smiles "that's weird" I shake my head and look at her "what?" She nods towards Brody's house and shrugs "his motorbike is gone already" she looks at her watch and shrugs "he usually doesn't leave until after half 8" I roll my eyes and buckle my belt in "ok time police" I smile and shrug "maybe he left early?" She does her belt and starts the car "yeah probably" she drives down the street and I look towards Brody's house as we drive past it and take a deep breath 'I hope he doesn't ask me what happened last night.' After Maths I have science and take my time walking there because I knew I would see Brody. I get too the classroom door and look in towards our desk but see no Brody 'weird' I shake my head and walk towards my desk and sit down waiting for the teacher to come in. After the final bell she rushes in and opens her laptop "eyes to the front please" she looks towards me and nods "I forgot Mr James wasn't in today" I look at Brody's empty seat and smile 'he isn't in today? What's going on' I look out the window and shake my head 'something feels off.' Mrs Luton pulls the projector down and I smile 'movie time' she starts a movie and I wait for her to turn the lights out and I rest my head on the table and look out the window 'where are you Brody and why are you not in school? Is it because of me? Has it got to do with Jeremy and last night?' I got so lost into my own thoughts that I didn't realise the time and the bell rang making me jump "class dismissed" I stand up and wait for the classroom to empty before approaching Mrs Luton "Mrs?" She looks at me and smiles "yes Amy" I look back towards my desk and shrug "why was Brody not in?" She looks at the desk and smiles softly "he was expelled yesterday" I raise my eyebrows and laugh nervously "what?" She nods firmly and smiles "he punched another student and was expelled for the rest of the week" I smile and shake my head "thank you" I take a deep breath and grab my bag "I got to go" I run out the door and run down the hallway towards the girl's bathroom. Shannon is in the bathroom fixing her lipstick but stops and looks at me when she spots me 'here we go' she looks back towards the mirror and wipes a bit of lipstick of her face and walks past me and out the door. I take a deep breath and shake my head before heading towards the mirror fixing my hair "only one more day until summer." I get my phone from my pocket and click on Brody's number 'please pick up!' After a few rings it goes to voicemail "dammit Brody" I take a deep breath and head out the bathroom and towards the front doors. I stop and look around when I get out and see Ryder standing by his bike, he waves at me when he spots me and smile "hey!" I smile and wave and walk towards him "hey." He looks around and shrugs "why you not in class?" I shrug and look down "I don't feel so good" he hands me his helmet and smirks "want a ride home?" I shrug and smile "that would be good thanks" I take the helmet and get on the back of the bike "why are you not in class?" He gets on and smiles "I have to get my sister for the dentist" I nod and hold onto him "ok" he drives of and heads towards my house. He pulls up outside and I spot Brody's motorbike by his house "I heard he got suspended and not allowed to attend the end of school dance" I shake my head and smile "really?" He looks at me and nods firmly "yeah because what he done with Ricky" I smile softly and look down "I should go" I look at his motorbike and wave "thanks for the ride" he gets back on his bike and smiles "anytime" I walk towards my house and wave "bye" he smirks and nods "bye Amy" he drives of down the street and I watch him as he disappears and head towards my house. I walk into the kitchen and bend down stroking Bear "hey boy!" He runs towards the back door so I walk towards it and unlock it letting him out. He runs around and I smile and shake my head "knock yourself out!" I grab a bottle of water from the fridge and head towards the kitchen window and see Brody walking out his shed holding a toolbox 'what is he building?' I smile and run towards the door and look at Bear "come on boy!" I see Brody looking at me with the side of my eye but looks back towards his house and disappears into his house without saying a word "rude much?" I scoff and shake my head "come on Bear" Bear runs in and I lock the door and run upstairs and into my room.

'How dare he ignore me!" I shake my head and stick my radio on 'never again!" I take a deep breath and walk towards the window and open my curtains and spot Brody in his bedroom hammering something 'hmm' I smirk and open my window a little and see him look up and smile a little before looking back down and continue to hammer 'I wonder if he's not speaking to me because Jeremy' I look over towards him and see him on the phone laughing before looking towards me and nodding 'weird.' I shake my head and run downstairs and head into the kitchen but stop when I hear my doorbell ring 'that best be Brody coming to say sorry for being rude' I walk towards the door and smile "yes?" I open the door and see Liam standing at the other side holding flowers "can I come in?" I nod and smile "of course" I open the door and he walks into the living room "these are for you" he hands me the big bunch of flowers and I smile and take them "what are these for?" I walk into the kitchen and he follows me laughing nervously "I kind of have bad news" I grab a vase from under the sink and place the flowers in them "what?" I look towards Brody's house and shake my head "is it to do with Jeremy?" Liam raises his eyebrow and shakes his head "what? No why would it have anything to do with Jeremy?" I look down and shake my head "no reason." He walks towards me and lifts my head up "has he said something to you?" I move my head away from his hand and shake it "no" he smiles softly and nods firmly "did he do something in the car last night?" I take a deep breath and shrug 'why did I have to open my big mouth?' Liam looks towards Brody's house and scoffs "that asshole!" He storms towards the door and shakes his head "I'm going to kill him!" I run after him and grab onto his arm "no Liam don't" he gets out the door with me hanging from his strong arm "what did he say?" I shake my head and attempt to dig my feet into the grass but he was too strong and I just slide across it "stop!" He stops at the fence and looks at me "what did he do Amy?" I shake my head and look down "he didn't DO anything it's what he said" I smile and shake my head "he told me to stay away from you and Brody" he looks towards Brody's house and shakes his head "why?" I look at him and shrug "I don't know" he walks towards me and wraps his arms around my shoulders and pulls me into him for a hug "he has always been protective but this is a new low even for him" I step away from him and shake my head "just don't cause a scene" he takes a deep breath and flings his head back "fine but I will be having a word with him later" I take a deep breath and nod "ok but stay calm" I shrug and look towards the house "I'm sure he has his reasons." He smiles and nods towards my house "come on" he walks into the house and sits down on the sofa and I follow and sit on the sofa across from him. He takes a deep breath and smiles "I'm leaving town" I shake my head and laugh nervously "what?" He shrugs and looks down "me and Jennifer are going back home" My smile disappears and I shake my head in disbelief "what? When?!" He looks down and shakes his head "tonight" he stands up and walks towards the window and looks out it "and when will youse be back?" He looks at me and shrugs "I don't know" I walk towards him and shake my head "so when will I see you again?" He sighs and shrugs "I don't know" I laugh nervously and he smirks "what?" I shake my head and walk toward the front door "bye Liam" he raises his eyebrow and shakes my head "what?" I look down towards the floor and shake my head "goodbye" he walks towards me and laughs nervously "are we not even going to talk about this?" I look at him and shrug "nothing to speak about" he walks out the door and looks back "I'm sorry" I smirk and shake my head "no I'm sorry" I shrug and hold onto the door tight "for thinking you was different!" I slam the door in his face before he can say another word and fix my dress and run upstairs and into my room closing the door behind me. 'What an ass!" I shake my head and star pacing my room "why would be ask me to be his girlfriend yesterday to just tell me he's leaving the next day?!" I grab something from my drawers and fling it without thinking or knowing what it was until it was too late. I hear a smash and look towards it and see a small hole in my window "great!" I shake my head and walk towards it and see glass on the floor under my window "Amy?!" I look out the window and see Brody leaning out his window "go away Brody!" I close my curtains and walk towards the hallway cupboard and grab the hoover. I walk towards the window and see the window blowing my curtains and I see into Brody's room and see Liam and Brody arguing, it looked more like Brody yelling at Liam 'wonder what they are arguing about' I smile and walk towards my window and try listen in "I knew you would do this!" I look out and see Liam looking towards the floor and Brody shaking his head at him "you should have stayed away from her and this would never have happened Liam!" I smile and lean more forward but I miss the window ledge and slip face first cutting my face and hands with the glass "ouch!" I cry out with pain as I feel the glass go into my face and feel the blood run down my face "Amy?!" I hear Liam and Brody call on my but I was in too much pain to sit up or call out back to them so I just lie there in the glass with blood running down my arms and face. I close my eyes and take a deep breath and sit up to scared to look at my arms or feeling my face, I run into the bathroom and run the warm watch and start pulling the pieces of glass out my arm and close my eyes and take a deep breath before looking into the mirror "ouch!" I look and see a piece of glass in my cheek "oh god" I shake my head and reach for it about to pull it out but stop when my bedroom door swings open "Amy?!" I run towards my bathroom door and slam it shut locking it "go away!" I hear Brody whispering "go get a towel" I hear footsteps run away and I step back from the door "Brody?" I hear him take a deep breath "yeah?" I shake my head and walk towards the mirror "go away." He laughs sarcastically "how bad is your face?" I shake my head and laugh nervously "don't know what you are talking about" I touch the largest piece of glass and pull it out "ouch!" I run the warm water over a cloth and stick it on my cheek but remove it when it stings my face making it worse 'wish Roxy wouldn't use my face cloths for her face wash' I look around and spot a new face cloth so I grab it and place it under warm water and place it on my cheek. "Here!" I look back towards the door and shake my head "youse can leave I'm fine!"

Liam tries the handle and sighs "come on Amy! Just come out" I walk towards the door and unlock the door and open it "happy?" They both look at my face and shake their heads "what happened?" I roll my eyes and walk past them onto my bed "I flung something and then heard youse arguing when I went to clean it up but I slipped and cut my face and arm" I hold my arm up which is still covered in glass and blood "let us help you get cleaned up?" Brody grabs the towel and I nod "fine" I look at Liam and sigh "but only because it stings really bad." Brody sits next to me and places the towel in his leg "let me see your arm" I place my arm on his leg and he runs his finger down my arm "Liam go get a bucket of warm water" Liam nods and runs into the bathroom and fills a bucket up with warm water and runs back in placing it on the floor in front of him "this might hurt a little" I nod my head and look away "go!" He starts to pull the pieces of glass out and I close my eyes and bite my bottom lip to stop me crying or punch him in the face. Liam walks towards my other side and holds my hand "you are going to be ok" I open my eyes and look at Liam and he smiles "just look at me" I can't help but smile as I look into his bright green eyes. With 1000 questions running through my head about why he was leaving and when or if he would be back I knew this wasn't the right time, not because Brody was here but because I was getting thousands of tiny little pieces of glass took out of my arm. I move my arm away from Brody's leg and he stands up "you want me to get the ones in your face?" I close my eyes and face Brody as he touches my face the pain feels like it's gone and even though I feel him taking the glass out it didn't hurt as much. He laughs softly and nods "that's you all done" I smile and open my eyes "thank you" I give him a hug and he laughs nervously and stands up "your welcome." He looks towards Liam and nods "I will leave youse two too it" he smile and walks towards the door "oh and Liam clean that up for her" he nods towards my window and Liam waves "I will" I smile and grab the hot wet face cloth and place it against my face "never ear dropping again" I laugh nervously and he smiles and lies back "I'm sorry" I lie back and look at him "I know" I shrug and laugh nervously "I'm sorry for not letting you explain yourself" I sit up and take a deep breath "I knew you wouldn't be in town long but it still sucks." He sits up and looks at me smirking "how did you know that I wouldn't be in town long?" I smile and nod towards the door "when Brody told me he had two cousin's he mentioned that they didn't stay in town but came to visit but didn't stay for long so when you came I should have known" he shrugs and lies back "I shouldn't have even let you get close to me without knowing I wouldn't be able to stay" I shake my head and raise my eyebrow "you tried to stay?" He nods and smiles "I'm 17 in 2 months so legally I don't need to go back into foster care and I can take Jennifer with me so I was hoping I could find a place here and we didn't have to move back but I didn't find a place" I smile and shake my head "why don't you just stay with Brody?" He stands up and walks towards the window grabbing the hoover "because I made a deal with the foster people that I would only move here if I got a job to provide for me and Jen" I smile and stand up "and you leave tonight?" He looks down and takes a deep breath "yeah why?" I shrug and walk towards the room door "so you still have a few hours" I nod towards the window and smirk "I might know a job for you" I run out the room and down the stairs into the kitchen grabbing Roxy's phone book and dialling a number "who you calling?" I stick my finger up and smile "hello can I speak too Craig please" I look at Liam and smile "hey Craig it's Amy" I laugh softly and nod "yeah" I look at Liam and cough "so Craig I have a favour" I smile and nod "my friend is looking for a job" I smirk and hold my thumb up towards Liam "ok thank you. Take care now, bye" I hang up and smile towards Liam "done" he shakes his head and walks towards me "so what's the job?" I write down on a piece of paper on Roxy's notebook and tear it of "it's in the garage in town" I shake my head and smile handing him the piece of paper "you know your way around cars right?" He takes the piece of paper and looks at it "yeah" he shakes his head and smirks "so just like that I got the job?" I shrug and smile "he owed me a favour" Liam raises his eyebrow "for what?" I roll my eyes and stand-up "I saved his daughter from falling down stairs" he hugs me and smiles "well aren't you a little super woman" he smiles and nods "I owe you one" I smirk and shrug "I know now go before it's too late" he smirks and nods "I will come back tonight with pizza to celebrate" I smile and nod "deal" he runs towards the front door and waves before leaving and closing it behind him. I grin from ear to ear and walk towards Bear "let's go for a walk" I grab his lead and grab my camera from the kitchen drawer and head towards the front door with Bear. I spot Jeremy getting into his car 'please don't notice me' he sticks his seat belt on and looks towards me and shakes his head "you!" He rolls his window down and leans out it "I warned you!" He looks towards his front door and shakes his head "this isn't over" he rolls his window back up and drives down the street 'I wish it was' I take a deep breath and walk down the stairs. "Hey!" I jump and look towards Brody's house and see him standing at his front door smiling "what was that about?" He nods towards the direction Jeremy drove of "what?" He looks at me and raises his eyebrow "what did Jeremy warn you about?" I shrug and look down "nothing" I walk past his gate and smile "bye" I speed walk down the street and out of his sight before he could say anything else 'why does Jeremy hate me so much?' I take a deep breath and shake my head 'screw him!' I turn into the wooden area and walk deeper into the woods before bending down and letting Bear of the lead "there you go boy" I smile at him as he shakes and sniffs the ground "come on!" I run of into the woods and he looks at me and barks before running after me "keep up!" I run faster looking behind me and see him running after me still before eventually catching up "good boy" I smile and bend down stroking his head and give him a dog treat. We walk deeper into the woods that I loose reception in my phone 'this is probably a good idea' I smile at Bear and nod "come on" I hold my camera up and aim it at him "pose for the camera" he jumps up and I capture it on camera "good boy" I smile and look around "perfect" I look towards an eagle in the tree above us and aim my camera towards it and take a picture "this place is amazing!" I look around and spot a light in between the tree's "come on boy" I walk towards it and bear follows me staying close. I get closer and spot a door and see the light coming out from there "what is this place?" I reach forward and the bush moves "it's sheets?" I shake my head and move them and see a door and a small shed "come on boy" I open the door and see stairs going down. I get my phone and see no signal still so I stick it back in my pocket and head down the stairs with Bear following closely behind me. At the bottom of the stairs I see a large black door with the letters 'Magnum' writing across it "where have I heard that name from?" I shake my head and open the door and it leads me into a small log cabin with white sheets over every piece of furniture and looking like the place hasn't been used or cleaned in years "stay close boy" I walk into the cabin closing the door behind me and head into the kitchen and see a newspaper from 10 years ago "Spies missing after being caught by local hero" I look at the picture and see a woman and man in there 30's and the woman had long beautiful ginger shiny hair and the man had black slick back hair. I stick the newspaper down and take a picture of the kitchen and spot a door at the side of the kitchen with a lock on it "wonder what's behind here" I walk towards it and pull the lock but it doesn't budge "whatever it is I'm guessing they didn't want anyone to find it." I head into the next room and it leads me into the living room where I look around and spot dusty photo frames on the fireplace "this is the spies house!" The people in the photo frames are the same people in the newspaper "oh shit!" I look around and shake my head "I wonder if this is where they came to hide?" I smile and look towards my camera "be rude not too" I take a few pictures and look towards the stairs "come on boy" I head towards the stairs and Bear follows behind me up every step. At the top of the stairs I come to a hallway with 2 rooms on each side "come on" I look behind me and see Bear struggling to get up the stairs "come on slow coach" I walk into the first room and see a bathroom with spider webs everywhere "nope" I quickly close the door behind me and head into the room opposite the bathroom "oh god what is that smell?" I smell a horrible odder, like gone of milk. I open the door and see a large bedroom with white sheets over the furniture "it's definitely in here!" I hold my nose and head towards the window and open it "hopefully that helps" I take a deep breath trying to get my smell back and look towards Bear as he walks slowly towards me "what is it boy?" He bends down ready to attack and jumps onto the bed dropping the white sheets of the bed making the smell worse "wow Bear!" I cover my face and shake my head laughing nervously "are you ok?" I look towards him and see a hand "Bear?!" He runs under the bed and I step back and shake my head "least I know what the smell is" I hold my nose again and walk towards the bed and look at the body on the bed and see the woman from the photo frame downstairs lying in bed dead, she looked like she had been there for years. Her skin had completely changed colour and she had bugs all around her face and body "ew!" I shake my head and run out the room "come on Bear." I head towards the stairs but stop when I hear a bang coming from downstairs "shhh"

I pick Bear up and quietly run down the hallway and into the last room and see another bedroom with white sheets everywhere. I head towards the bed and hide under it holding Bear in my hands, he starts to growl so I stroke his head still locking my eyes onto the door and take a deep breath "shh boy." Bear manages to escape out my arms and runs out from under the bed "no Bear!" I quickly get out and bend down and pick him up but he moves and I lose my balance and fall onto the bed hitting something hard "oh god that smell again" I shake my head and stand up taking a deep breath "please be a bag of milk that has went off" I take the covers of the bed and see the other spy from the photo frame "eww!" I quickly stick the sheet back over them and look towards the door "so who's downstairs?" I grab Bear and take a deep breath "come on." I head towards the stairs and look down and see a rat on the fireplace eating something "it's only a rat." I take a deep breath and look towards Bear "come on" I look around the cottage and smile "that's enough adventure for one day." I walk towards the door we came from and pull it "it's locked" I look at Bear and laugh nervously "let's try the front door" I walk into the living room and walk towards the front door and try open it "this is also locked!" I look around and head into the kitchen "come on" I look in the drawers and find a set of keys "bingo!" I smile and pick them up and see an envelope under them with my address on it "what is this?" I shake my head and pick up the envelope and open it "it's" I look at the piece of paper and shake my head "it's the map to the secret rooms at the house!" I smirk and shake my head "they actually exist?" I stick the pieces of paper back into the envelope and stick it in my bag before grabbing the keys and head out the front door. I head back through the forest and hear my phone ding a few times when I get back into the open area 'I'm guessing Roxy is home' I pull my phone out my pocket and see missed calls and text messages from Liam and Brody "come on boy!" I look towards Bear and smile before running through the woods towards the exit. I get home and stick my camera on the kitchen table and see Brody in his back yard with Jennifer so I walk towards the back door and open it "hey youse!" Brody jumps up and looks over with a white face like he has just seen a ghost "where have you been?" I shake my head and smile "out taking photos why?" He grabs his phone and rings someone "Liam was looking for you" I smile and nod "I know I seen the missed calls but I just got back so I will ring him now." Brody waves towards the side of my house and smirks "no need" he comes of the phone and I look towards the side of my house and see Liam come around the corner smirking "hey you!" I smile and wave "hello" he runs towards me and hugs me "I got the job and start tomorrow so thank you so much I owe you" I laugh softly and hug him "so you can stay?" He nods and smile "I can stay" I smile and nod firmly "good" I shrug and shove him softly "you're the only real friend I have here so would be a bummer if you left" he hugs me and smiles "back at ya!" Jennifer and Brody come over laughing "so it's you I have to thank for us staying?" I look at Jennifer and nod "I guess so" she smiles and runs towards me smiling "thank you!" I hug her and laugh softly "your welcome." She looks at Liam and shrugs "Liam should take you to the dance Saturday as a way to say thank you" I look at Liam and shrug "I wasn't planning on going but it could be fun if you came?" He smirks and nods firmly "I would love to" I nod and run towards my back door "I need a dress then" I smirk and wave "bye" I run into the house closing the door behind me. I run upstairs and look in my drawers "dress dress dress" I sigh and shake my head sitting back "hey!" I Jump and turn around and see Roxy standing by my room door smirking "did you say dress?" I smile and nod "I need a dress for this school dance Saturday" She grins and nods "this way" I stand up and follow her towards her closet "help yourself" she turns the closet light on and I look around and smile "I don't even know where to start." She holds up a long red dress with a slit in the leg "this could work" she smiles and nods toward my room "go try it on and I will find you more" I nod and smile "ok" I walk towards my room and sit the dress on the bed 'let's get this over with.' I try on the dress as Roxy walks in holding a bundle of other dresses "help!" I look down at the dress and see my boob half hanging out and the slit in the middle of the dress nearly revealing my pants "come here" she walks towards me and fix's the dress and smiles "there." I walk towards the mirror hanging at the back of my bathroom door and smirk "I don't like the slit" I look towards the slit and shake my head "what's next?" She hands me another dress and I take it and smile "thank you." The rest of the evening I try on loads of different dresses and eventually pick one I like, a peachy pink colour dress with a lace top and a slit at the back. I smile and shake my head "this is the one" I look into the mirror and see Jeremy standing by my room door smirking "god!" I jump and turn around "oh hey Jeremy" Roxy stands up and smiles "I'm going for dinner with Jeremy so you ok ordering pizza?" I smile and nod "of course" she hugs me and smiles "you're the best." She walks out the room and I look at Jeremy and roll my eyes 'here we go' he looks towards the stairs and looks back at me "nice dress" he looks me up and down and smirks "so I heard you're going to the dance with Jeremy?" I smirk and nod "yes so?" I cross my arms and look him up and down "hmm" I roll my eyes and walk towards the door "bye" I close the door in his face and fling my head back "what's his problem?" I sigh and shake my head "weirdo!" I walk towards my drawers and get pj's out and smile "night in my pj's and pizza sounds perfect" I place the peachy dress on the bottom of my bed and lift the other dresses up and stick them back in Roxy's cupboard. "Bye!" I look down the stairs and see Roxy and Jeremy heading out the door "bye" I look at Jeremy and smirk "I'm going to invite Jeremy over if you don't mind?" I look at Roxy and she smiles "of course not" she points at me and raises her eyebrows "but behave" I roll my eyes and lean over the stairs railing "we are just friends" Jeremy nods and smiles "let's go" Roxy nods and waves "bye" I wave and she closes the door behind her. "Like I am going to invite anyone over" I walk into my bathroom and grab a face mask "this is the perfect night" I grab the face mask and my earphone's and head downstairs sticking on the TV and placing the face mask and earphones on the sofa "cucumber" I smile and head into the kitchen opening the fridge and grabbing the cucumber and knife and cut 2 slices before looking towards the cupboards "now snacks" I look around the cupboards grabbing a few snacks and a large bottle of cola "now I'm ready." I head into the living room and place everything on the sofa and close the curtains and walk towards the front door and lock it "no one will be disturbing me and Chris Hemsworth tonight" I smirk and look towards Bear sitting behind me "you coming?" He barks and runs towards me "take that as a yes" I smirk and walk into the living room and turn the lights of before sitting down lifting Bear up next to the sofa next to me and grab my facemask. I stick the facemask on and look at Bear smirking "and relax" I play the DVD and lean back watching it. After half an hour I feel myself starting to drift of but jump when someone presses my doorbell making me wide away "who can that be?" I look at my phone and shake my head "it's 8PM" I sigh and pause the move and get up before walking towards the door "who is it?" I look through the keyhole and see Jennifer standing at the other side "it's Jennifer" I smile and open the door "hey." She smirks at me trying to hold her laughter in that her face goes red "I still have this face mask on don't I?" She laughs softly and nods "yeah" I shake my head and look down "please come in" she smiles as I open the door wide and she walks in "thank you." She walks into the living room and spots Bear sleeping on the sofa "Liam told me you had Bella's brother" I smile and look at him "I know what are the chances" she looks at me and smiles "so I just wanted to come by and give you something" she goes into her bag and pulls out a little red box "it was my mums." I take it and open it "it's beautiful" I look at the lovely silver diamond bracelet "it's for you" I close it and shake my head handing it back to her "I can't accept this" she shakes her head and smiles "at least keep it until Sunday? You can wear it to the dance Saturday" I smile and nod "fine." I stick it on top of the cabinet "thank you" she hugs me and smiles "your welcome" I hug her back and smile "you should get back before they send a search party out" she nods and laughs nervously "true." She walks towards the door and waves "bye" I smile and wave as she opens the front door "bye" she closes the door behind her and I walk towards it and lock it. I sit back on the sofa and open a bag of Cheetos before playing the movie again cuddling into Bear as he sleeps "hopefully no more interruptions this time" I watch the rest of the movie but drift of too sleep halfway through it.

I wake up the next morning in bed 'how did I get here?' I get up and walk towards Roxy's room and see her still sleeping "Roxy?" She pulls the covers back over her head "no!" I roll my eyes and laugh softly "fine I will get myself to school" I close her door leaving it open a little and head back into my bedroom and get dressed. I sit on the side of my bed and stick my shoes on and look at my alarm clock and sigh "8.15" I nod and stand up "still got time for breakfast." I run downstairs and see Bear standing in the kitchen wagging his tail "hey boy!" He runs towards me and jumps up licking my hand "you want breakfast?" He barks and I laugh softly and shake my head "shh! Roxy is still sleeping" I grab his bowl and fill it with dog foot and grab a cereal bar and a bottle of water and head towards the door "bye Bear!" I head down the stairs and see Jeremy outside his front door having a jag leaning against the door "hey!" He smirks at me but I shake my head and keep walking down the path towards the gate "Roxy still sleeping then?" He walks towards his car and nods "want a ride?" I look at the car and smirk "I'm good thanks." He looks up and shrugs "but it's raining" I look up at the grey sky and shake my head "no it's" before I could finish that sentence the rain pours down, hard and cold. It soaks me within 5 seconds and I look at Jeremy who has the biggest grin on his face "I would still rather walk" I close the gate behind me and start walking down the street towards school. Jeremy gets in his car and drives slowly the side of the pavement beside me "Amy just get in!" I stop and look around "fine but don't speak" he nods and unlocks the car "deal." I get in the passenger side and he drives of fast before I get my belt on "so" I look at him and shake my head "don't speak I said" he nods firmly and looks towards the road "fine." He sticks the radio and whistles along to the song "if I was allowed to speak I would say sorry" I raise my eyebrows and look at him confused "what?" He looks at me and shrugs "I got you wrong" I roll my eyes and lean back "ok." He raises his eyebrow and laughs softly "that's it?" I shrug and look at him "yeah" he nods firmly and smirks "ok then." He pulls into the school car park and I shake my head "I can just get out here" he drives into the car park and stops "I'm sorry" I shake my head and scoff "for what part?" He looks down at his feet "I thought you was" he takes a deep breath and smiles "pretending to be someone else" I laugh nervously and grab my bag "ok bye" he touches my arm and smiles "it's ok" I look at him and he nods firmly "Roxy told me everything" I raise my eyebrows and smirk "did she now?" He moves his arm and nods "she told me about Nathan and what he done" I grab my bag and open the door "I don't want to talk about it!" I slam the door and run into the school entrance and straight to the bathroom 'he's got to be lying? Roxy would never tell a man she has only known a few days about Nathan?' I grab my phone and text her 'Ring me when you see this x' I take a deep breath and head out the bathroom. "Hey!" I jump when I see Ryder standing at the door smirking "morning" I smile and nod "morning" he wraps his arm around mine and nods "come on" I shake my head and laugh "where you taking me?" He heads down the hallway smirking "you will see." I follow him into the gym and he nods towards the basketball hoop and I see a sign "Will you go to the End of School dance with me?" I look at Ryder and smirk "that's so sweet" I look down and sigh "but I'm already doing with someone" he raises his eyebrow and shakes his head "what? But how? Brody's been expelled from going" I smile and look at him "I know" I shrug and laugh nervously "I'm going with his cousin instead." He raises his eyebrow and laughs sarcastically "Liam?" I nod and smile "yeah why?" He shrugs and shakes his head smirking "nothing." I smile softly and rub his arms "you going to be ok?" He nods and wraps his arm around mine "yeah" he smiles and nods towards the gym exit door "come on." I follow him out the gym and he spots Ricky "I will see you in English?" I smile and nod "ok" he runs over to Ricky and I take a deep breath 'that wasn't awkward at all' I shake my head and walk towards English. I get to the classroom just as the bell rings so I sit down and see Ryder walk in as the final bell rings, I smile and wave and he nods towards me and looks back towards the door and I see Abbie walk in laughing at him rubbing his arm 'he didn't!' I look down trying to hold my laughter in as he walks towards me "hey" I look up and smile "hi" he looks back towards Abbie and nods "I'm going to sit with Abbie if you don't mind?" I look over towards her and see her playing with her hair smirking towards me "no I don't mind" he nods and grins "ok thanks" he walks towards her and sits down 'unbelievable' I shake my head and look towards the teacher as she walks in the classroom. The rest of the day I watch movies in every class and my last class is science where we watch the rest of Frankenstein, at the end of the class Mrs Luton calls me over and hands me an envelope "give this too Brody please" I stick it in my bag and nod "ok." I walk towards the exit and see Ryder standing by his locker with Abbie "Amy!" I look over and see him waving towards me "I got to go Abbie but I will see you tomorrow for dress shopping" he runs over towards me and smirks "you excited?" I shake my head and look down "for what?" He wraps his arm around mine and smiles "for school to be over for the next few weeks" I shrug and laugh nervously "not really" I look at him and smile "before this I didn't go to school so it's nice to go for a change" he scoffs and shakes his head "well I will be happy to see the back of it and enjoy the best summer." He looks around and shakes his head "no Roxy?" I look around and shake my head "I guess not" he smirks and nods towards his bike "let me drop you of?" I smirk and nod "ok." We walk towards his bike and he hands me the helmet "so my dad has this lake house just outside town and I'm planning a party Saturday after the dance if you want to come?" He shrugs and shakes his head "can even bring Liam" I stick the helmet on and get on the back of the bike "sounds fun" he drives of and I grip tightly onto him. He pulls up outside and I spot Roxy looking out the living room window waving "thank you" I get of the bike and hand Ryder the helmet and he waves at Roxy and smiles "your welcome." I walk towards the house and see Roxy smirking "what?" She shakes her head and walks into the kitchen "nothing." I follow her in and shake my head "so what happened last night with Jeremy?" She laughs nervously and looks in the cupboard's "what do you mean?" I raise my eyebrow and walk towards her "he told me he knew about Nathan?" She takes a deep breath and nods "I had to tell him" I shake my head and scoff "why? Did he threaten you?" She closes the cupboard door and shakes her head "no it wasn't like that" she looks at me and smiles softly "the school couldn't find your medical records and the receptionist at the school is friends with Jeremy so he called him and said because he thought something was of but I explained last night." I smile and look towards the floor "so that's why he was acting weird the other day" Roxy laughs nervously and nods "yeah he told me about that and said he was really sorry." I grab an apple from the fruit bowl and nod "I know he dropped me of at school earlier and said sorry." I walk towards the door and look back towards Roxy and smile "he's not the worse you know" I eat into the apple and walk upstairs and into my room. I take my jacket of and hang it on the back of the door and shake my head "I wish Roxy wouldn't have the heating on so high" I laugh softly and walk towards my window and open it. I look out the window and see Jennifer and Bella in Brody's back garden "hey!" I smile and she looks up and waves "hi!" I nod towards Bella and smirk "you want a puppy play date?" She stands up and nods "yeah!" I nod and wave "ok I will go get Bear" I run downstairs and open the back door "come on boy" Bear jumps up from his bed and runs out the back yard "where you going?" I nod towards Brody's house and smile "having a play date with the dogs" she laughs softly and shakes her head "have fun" I nod and smile "I will" I close the door behind me and run towards the fence in between the houses. I stick Bear down and climb the fence and walk towards Jennifer and sit down "hey" she smiles and looks up "hi." Bear and Bella run of and Jennifer hands me a can of cola "thanks" I open the drink and take a sip "so you fancy my brother?" I nearly choke on my drink and laugh nervously wiping my mouth "what?" She laughs softly and shrugs "it's ok if you do" she looks down and smirks "your nice" she looks at me and I blush "thank you but no me and Liam are just friends." She sighs and nods firmly "shame" I smirk and shake my head "so are you glad that youse don't need to leave?" t nods and smiles "yeah" she stands up and looks towards Bella "I believe I have you to thank?" I nod and stand up "your brother was so nice to me and I didn't want him to leave" she smirks and shakes his head "why are youse not together" I roll my eyes and smirk "because friends seem better" I shrug and laugh softly "I've never had a good friend so It's nice and I don't want to lose that" she nods firmly and smiles "what about Brody?" The door behind us opens and I look over and see Brody standing with no top on leaning against the door smirking "what about me?" Jennifer rolls her eyes and looks at me "maybe next time we can do this at yours?" I smirk and nod "agreed." I walk towards the fence and look towards Bear "come on boy!"

He runs towards me and I lift him up and climb the fence and walk towards the door looking at Brody still smirking at me before heading inside. I head into the living room and see Roxy lying on the sofa "you really that hungover still at 4PM?" She attempts to lift her head up and laughs "yeah" I laugh softly and shake my head "pizza?" She sighs and flings her hand up "hmmm!" I grab the blanket from the cupboard in the hallway and cover her with it "I'm going to try get more photos so I will leave you too it." I grab my camera from the unit and head towards the door "I will bring pizza back" I look towards the kitchen and smile "you coming Bear?" Bear looks up and barks and runs towards me "come on then" I open the door and close it behind me and walk towards the woods. After what feels like an hour I look at the sky as it starts to get dark and smile "we should head back" I look at Bear and he lies down on the ground panting "its" I look at my phone and laugh nervously "9PM?!" I shake my head and scoff "let's go." We head back out towards the street and I hear my phone ding a few times one after another "that will be

Roxy awake" I grab my phone and see Roxy sent me 8 text messages and 4 messages from Brody "I bet she has got the search party out" I laugh softly and open the messages from Brody "where are you?" I scoff and shake my head "Amy where are you? Roxy is freaking out" I stick my phone back into my pocket and look towards bear "let's go." I start running through the woods and bear follows behind me, I stop when I get back into the street and look up towards my house and see Roxy outside with Jeremy "someone doesn't look happy" I look I Bear and smirk "let's get this over with." We walk towards her and after a few seconds she looks towards me and grins in relief "Amy!" She runs towards me and I shake my head "what? I was only gone about 4 hours?" She grabs me in for a cuddle "you didn't tell me where you was going and I got worried when I woke up and Jeremy said he saw you leave at 4 so I got worried" I shake my head and hug her "I'm fine" I show her my camera and smirk "I was out taking more pictures and took Bear for a walk" she looks towards Bear and laughs nervously "I didn't even think about that." She looks towards the camera and shakes her head smirking "you could have at least told me" I smirk and nod "I did!" I wrap my arm around hers and walk towards the house "come on you." I see Jeremy looking at me smiling "shall we call the search party of then?" I smirk and nod "yes please." He looks towards the house and laughs nervously "oi!" He looks at me and smiles 'who else has she got looking for me?' I look towards the door and see Brody and Liam appear when the door open "Amy!" They run towards me smiling before cuddling me "where have you been? Are you ok?" I nod firmly and laugh "I am fine!" I look at Roxy and shake my head "she just passed out and must have forgotten I told her I was going out." Brody looks to Bear and smiles "I told you she would be out with the dog" Liam shakes his head and points towards my camera "but she also had her camera" I roll my eyes and walk towards my house "bye guys" I open the gate and look at Bear "come on boy!" He runs in and I close the gate and look at Roxy "I'm going to bed" she nods and smiles "ok." She looks at Jeremy and sighs "I should go" he kisses her and I shake my head "gross!" I walk towards the door and leave it open behind me and run upstairs into my room. I place my camera on my drawers and get a hair band and tie my hair up before heading into the bathroom 'a nice warm shower will be perfect right now' I run the shower and grab a clean towel before closing the bathroom door a little and getting undressed. After the shower I head into my bedroom and see Roxy sitting on my bed "hey" I walk towards her towel drying my hair "what's up?" She looks down and smirks "so this no boys rule" I roll my eyes and look towards my window "I think that rule is broken" she looks at me and smirks "I thought so." She stands up and takes the wet towel from me and walks towards the door "just be careful" I look at her and smile softly "I will don't worry" she waves and smiles "night" I nod and wave back at her "goodnight" before turning the light of and getting into bed.

"WAKE UP!" Roxy runs into my room screaming "what?!" I quickly jump up still half asleep and grab the closest thing to me "what's happened?" She laughs and takes the object from my hand "nothing but what you going to do? Let Mr P cuddle them?" I see my penguin teddy from when I was a child in her hands "yeah." I take it of her and stick it on my bed "what you going all crazy for? What's happened?" She shrugs and smiles "it's the last day of school" I roll my eyes and fall onto my bed "really?" She walks towards me and sits down "well I'm excited for you since you have never experienced it." I sit up and smile "I am more excited for taking time to take more photos and build up my portfolio for college." She looks towards my wall where my pictures are and nods "you will smash it." She stands up and nods towards my alarm clock "I will be down stairs with breakfast" I smile and nod "Ok I am going to get dressed" she looks towards my window and smirks "well don't try look to cute" she smirks and shrugs "Brody won't be there" I fling Mr P towards her and laugh nervously "you're the worst!" She catches him and smirks "so you do like him? I knew it!" She flings him back towards me and runs of downstairs "I do not!" I stand up and close the door slightly and grab clothes and get ready. I walk into the kitchen with my hair wrapped up in a messy bun "can you drop me of?" I see Roxy looking towards the table before looking at me "no." I walk into the kitchen and spot Liam "hey!" He stands up and hugs me "I will drop you of and we can talk about tomorrow" I nod firmly and smile "ok well let's go" I walk towards the front door and grab my school bag and open the front door "come on!" I look behind me and see Liam laughing "I'm coming!" He waves towards Roxy and follows me out the door. I look around and smile "so what one is yours?" He laughs sarcastically and shakes his head running down the stairs "we are not taking my car." He walks towards Brody's fence and nods "we are taking Brody's" I look at Brody's motorbike and sigh "his bike? I can hardly hear myself think on that thing never mind us talk about tomorrow" he rolls his eyes and climbs the fence "good thing we are going for breakfast first then" he smirks and I nod "that works" I walk towards the fence and climb it and get onto the back of the motorbike holding onto Liam. He pulls into a café carpark and stops "come on." He gets off and helps me down "I'm parched" I laugh softly and follow him into the café. We sit down and I look at the menu and stick it down after two seconds "so what did you want to discuss?" He sticks his menu down and smiles "outfits, how we get there, after plans?" I smile and nod "ok." I go into my bag and grab my notebook "well I am wearing a peachy coloured dress and we can get Roxy to drop us of?" He looks out the window and smirks "or we could take the motorbike?" I laugh sarcastically and shake my head "definitely not." I look at my phone and smirk "and there is an after party going on at Ryders and we got an invite" he raises his eyebrow and smirks "we?" I smile and nod "yes we." He shrugs and leans back "alright then" he grabs the menu and smirks "now for food" I pick my menu up and smirk shaking my head.

After breakfast Liam drops me of at school and smiles "see you tomorrow then?" I nod and hand him his helmet "see you tomorrow" he smirks and sticks the helmet on before waving and driving off. I look towards the floor as I walk towards the school but stop when I see two shadows in front of me "oh sorry" I try to move past but they move the same time "excuse me" I look up and see Abbie and Shannon smirking "move!" Abbie pushes past me making me drop my school bag "rude bitch!" I bend down and grab my school bag and see her feet stop and turn around "play fair Abbie!" I stand up and see Ryder grabbing onto Abbie's arm as she holds a bottle of water in it "whatever!" She pulls her arm away and turns around storming of "you ok?" I nod and smile "yeah." I look towards Abbie and shake my head "thanks." Ryder looks at me and smirks "anytime" he wraps his arm around mine and smiles "come on" he walks towards the school and I follow behind him. "We don't even have a half day" I look at Ryder and smile nervously "what do mean?" He nods towards the gym hall and smirks "we have to attend this assembly then we can go home" I roll my eyes and scoff "well I didn't know that" he smirks and opens the gym door "you need a ride home?" I smile and nod "that would be fab thanks" I walk into the gym and see loads of chairs set out so I follow Ryder and sit down. "You excited for tomorrow?" I nod and smile "yeah are you?" He laughs softly and nods "yes but not looking forward to cleaning Sunday morning." I smirk and shrug "I can help if you like?" He looks at me and his eyes shoot with excitement "really? That would be great" he leans back and shrugs "the house has enough bedrooms so you can have a sleep too if you like?" I smile and nod "sounds like a plan." Miss June the head teacher walks in and everyone cheers and claps as she walks towards the microphone "alright alright" she sticks her hand up and everyone stops and sits back down "I won't keep youse long" she smiles and looks around "I know youse have a dance to get prepared for tomorrow so I just wanted to say thank you to everyone for making this the best year and I hope youse have all the best time tomorrow night and have the best summer!" Everyone around me stands up and claps including Ryder "yes!" I laugh softly and stand up and clap "come on" Ryder grabs my hand and heads towards the exit pushing past people. "Finally summer starts" I laugh sarcastically as I get onto Ryders motorbike "yeah not seeing me for the next few weeks will be good" he hands me a helmet and smirks "who said I won't see you?" He gets on the bike and laughs nervously "you are not getting rid of me that easily Amy" he starts the bike and I hold tightly onto him as he drives of fast. He pulls up outside my house and I see Jeremy and Roxy speaking in the living room "are they dating?" I look at Ryder and see him looking at the window "I think so" I shrug and hand him the helmet back "not sure." He smiles and sticks the helmet on the seat "you want to grab breakfast? They look pretty busy" I look back towards the window and see them kissing and Jeremy taking Roxy's t-shirt of "sounds good!" He hands me the helmet back and I quickly get back onto the bike and he drives of down the street. Ryder pulls up outside a little burger place called 'Burger Bun' and smiles "this is the best place in town." I get of the bike and nod "its 9AM" I look at him and smirk "is it even open?" He walks towards the door and pulls out keys "it is when your dad owns it" I follow him in and smile "I hope you can cook." He locks the door behind us and heads towards the kitchen "come on" I follow him in and I see two burger meals on the counter "yeah I can't cook but I got one of the workers to come in" he nods towards a door at the side of the kitchen and I look over and see a man holding a clipboard "was trying to impress you" he holds me the burger and I smirk and take it "food is a way to a woman's heart so I have heard." I eat a bite into my burger and Ryder looks at me and smirks "I will need to keep that in mind" I nod and smirk "good." I walk towards the doors into the seating area and nod "come on" Ryder follows me and I sit down and he grabs two drinks from the fridge and joins me handing me a bottle of cola "thank you." I look around and smile "so your dad owns this place?" Ryder eats the rest of his burger and nods "he owns another 6 around the country so he is hardly here" I shrug and lean forward "must make you proud though?" He leans back and shrugs "I guess." He stands up and smiles "let's go" I stand up and follow him out the door and towards his motorbike "where are we going?" He hands me the helmet and I get on the back and stick it on "a drive" he gets on and starts the engine and I hang onto him. After half an hour he stops at the side of a lake with an of road path "I used to come here a lot with my dad" he smiles and nods "hold on" I hold onto him and he drives through the woods and up the of road. He eventually stops again and gets of the bike "ready?" I get of the bike and hand him the helmet "for what?" He nods behind me so I turn around and see the most beautiful waterfall falling into a large clear blue steam "wow." I move closer and look over the edge "you can see the fish from here" he walks towards me and smirks "my dad used to bring me here every summer for fishing." He looks down and sighs "I am happy for him that he is extending his business but he is never here and It sucks" I smile softly and rub his arm "I can imagine" he looks at me and smirks "I'm sorry!" He shakes his head and laughs nervously "there's my banging on about not being able to spend enough time with my dad and you can't see your dad again" I laugh softly and shake my head "its fine I get it, it sucks." He smirks and nods "let's get you back home before the rain starts" I look up and see the clouds turn grey "good idea" he hands me the helmet and I stick it on and get on the back of the bike and he drives of. After a while he pulls up outside my house and I see Liam and Brody standing outside Brody's door speaking "Amy?" I look over and wave "hey." Liam looks at Brody and he shakes his head and smile "what?" Ryder laughs softly and looks down "think someone is jealous" he looks up and I laugh nervously and shake my head "Liam? No we are just friends" I look towards them and smile "not Liam" Ryder looks at them and smirks "Body." I shake my head and smirk "no way he hates me" I look back and see Brody looking me up and down before heading back inside "I'm telling you" I look at him and smirk "he's into you." I hand him his helmet back and smile "thank you for the burger" he nods and waves "anytime" he sticks the helmet on and starts the engine "bye" he drives of and I wave and turn around and head into the house. I run into my room and star fight my bed taking a deep breath 'why would Ryder say that about Brody? Brody doesn't give me that vibe at all' I stand up and look out the window towards Brody's house and sigh "snap out of it" I shake my head and walk towards the window closing the curtains and walk back towards my bed and star fish it. I close my eyes and take a deep breath "boys!" I hear someone knocking on my door making me jump "only me." Roxy walks in smiling "hi" I sit up and smirk "hey." She sits next to me and nods "what are you not at school?" I nod firmly "we only had to go in to attend an assembly" she nods and smiles firmly "so who has annoyed you now?" I laugh softly and shake my head "just something Ryder said." She sits back and crosses her legs "want to talk about it?" I look towards my window and shrug "he said that Brody likes me?" Roxy stays silent and looks down "what?" She looks at me and shakes her head "and you don't think he does?" I raise my eyebrows and scoff "no!" I look down and blush "why do you?" She laughs softly and stands up "do you want him too?" I shrug and look at her "I never thought about it" I stand up and walk towards the window opening the curtains "I mean he's hot and he is super sweet" I blush and smirk before looking at Roxy "but he's always hot and cold and he is really mysterious." Roxy nods and smiles "sounds like he is trying to test the waters" I raise my eyebrow and laugh nervously "what does that mean?" She shakes her head and smirk "he is checking if you like him back before he puts himself out there" I smile and look back out the window "I don't know how I feel yet" I shrug and sigh "I always thought that once you knew you knew" I look at Roxy and nod "you know?" She rolls her eyes and scoffs "you have been watching too many romantic movies" she walks towards the door and waves "I'm going to work" I smile and wave "have fun" she nods and smiles "always do" she walks out the door and I look back towards Brody's window again before taking a deep breath "I guess there is only one way to find out" I smirk and close the curtains and head towards my bed and lie down closing my eyes before drifting off to sleep.

I wake up a few hours later and realise the sun was setting "oh shit!" I quickly stand up and run out the room and downstairs "Roxy?" I walk into the kitchen Bear jumps up and runs towards me "hey boy!" I see money and a note on the table so I open the letter and smile "I'm away out with Jeremy and didn't want to wake up so left money for pizza. See you soon love Rox" I nod firmly and grab the money "pizza on Roxy it is." I grab the phone and dial the pizza company and order myself a large pizza before heading back upstairs grabbing my school bag and emptying it onto the bed. My books all fall out so I grab them and place them in a box from under my bed and look back onto my bed and see the envelope from the cabin in the woods 'I forgot about this' I open it and look at the map "so this is" I grab the envelope and run downstairs into the kitchen and look towards the back door "this is there" I see a door on the map and smile "so the secret room is" I look back towards the map and smile "there!" I look out towards the back garden and smirk "let's go and check it out then boy" Bear barks and follows me out the back garden and towards the grass. I look at the map again and sigh "ok so" I look around the grass and smirk "is that it?" I look back at the map and see a 'X' right where I am standing so I bend down and feel the grass "this feel's fake?" I look at Bear and he tilts his head "wait I can feel something." I feel a hatch handle so I pull it and sigh "nothing" I look at the map and nod firmly "what if I" I push the hatch handle and it makes a noise "wow!" The ground goes into the grass and a ladder appears to go down "you coming?" Bear lies down and I shrug "your loss" I look back towards the ladder and take a deep breath "here goes." I climb down the ladder and grab my phone as I reach the bottom of darkness "no lights? Typical" I shine my light around and see a switch at the side of the ladder "maybe this is?" I turn it on and lights appear "perfect!" I turn my torch on my phone of and look around the dusty room filled with TV screens and a large keyboard "what?" I walk towards the keyboard and press the power button and all the TV's turn on "it's a CCTV room?" I look at the TV's and see each room in the house on them "cool!" I spot Brody on one of the cameras by my front door "oh no!" I look at the camera on the back garden and see Bear stand up and run into the house "how do I get this ladder up!" I quickly walk towards the ladder and see a red button behind it so I press it and the ladder folds up and closes "that will be how." I look back towards the cameras and see Brody looking around and mouthing "I wonder if I can hear them" I look at the keyboard and see a mute button so I press it and hear Bear barking "wow too loud!" I quickly turn it down a little and sigh "better." I look back towards the screen Brody is on and see him grabbing his phone out and ringing someone "no she isn't answering so I'm guessing she is still sleeping but I will check again in an hour" he looks back towards the door and nods firmly "ok bye Jer" he hangs up and heads back towards his house. I take a deep breath and look around "what else have you got down here?" I see a set of drawers so I walk towards it and try open it but its locked "typical!" I look around and grab the envelope and reach into it and smirk when I feel a key "bingo!" I try the key into the lock and it clicks "I'm getting good at this" I open the drawer and see a black folder so I grab it and sit down by the keyboard and place the folder on the table and open it "File number 4 The Secret powers of Kalispell" I smirk and shake my head and laugh nervously "ok then." I look back at the folder and keep reading "Are there people living among us with abnormal abilities? Can people fly? Have super strength? Or maybe even be able to blow a house down by one single blow?" I laugh sarcastically and shake my head "and these people was real spies?" I scoff and shake my head "no wonder they got fired!" I look back towards the folder but jump when I hear a door slam closed 'Roxy!' I look towards the screens and see Roxy stumble in taking her shoes of "Amy?!" She looks into the living room and stops for a few seconds "are you awake?" I shake my head and sigh "someone is drunk" I close the folder and head back towards the ladder and head up quickly feeling around until I find a button "there!" I press the button and look down the ladders and see them come up and the fake grass sets back into place. I look towards the house and see Roxy's room light turn on so I nod and run into the kitchen locking the door behind me "Amy?" I run into the hallway and look upstairs "yeah?" Roxy runs down the stairs and laughs softly "hey you!" I laugh nervously and shake my head "how much have you had to drink?" She starts counting with her fingers and shrugs "a lot?" I nod and smile "ok well you go to bed and I will bring you up some water" she smirks and nods "thank you" I nod and she walks back upstairs. I walk into the kitchen and grab a glass and walk towards the sink and pour a glass looking out the window towards the secret room "I cannot believe it actually exists" I stop the water and turn around dropping the glass when I see Jeremy standing behind me "what exists?" I shake my head and get the brush set "what?" He stumbles into the kitchen and I smirk 'he's drunk. You got this!' I clean up the glass and stick it in the bin "I just seen a white owl and didn't know they were real" he raises his eyebrows and walks towards the fridge grabbing two bottles of water continue" I nod and smile as he walks upstairs "ok then!" I grab a glass and pour water into it and head upstairs and get into bed turning my bedside lamp on and reach for my camera and laptop and start uploading the photos from my camera onto my laptop. I stick the laptop too the side of my while it uploads and lie back onto the bed and sigh "what a day!" I look at the laptop and shake my head "I should really do this as soon as I take the pictures" I close my eyes and after a few minutes I drift off to sleep. I get woken up again when my laptop dings and quickly sit up and look around before rubbing my eyes and yawning "eventually" I close my laptop and stick my camera and it on my bedside table before turning my lamp of and going under my covers and drifting of back to sleep.

The next morning I wake up with Roxy running into my room holding a large makeup bag "it's the day of the dance!" She sits down beside me and smirks "let's get you ready!" I shake my head and look at my alarm clock "its 11AM what are you doing?" She looks at the clock and turns it over "it's never too early to get ready for an important dance" I smile and fling the covers of me "hit me with your best shot" she smirks and stands up squirming in excitement "let's get ready!!!" She runs into the bathroom and grabs a towel and flings me it "go for a shower and I will prepare everything" I stand up and nod "ok boss" she laughs sarcastically and places the makeup bag on my bed "about time you admit that I'm boss." I roll my eyes and head into the bathroom and start the shower "make sure you don't flood the bathroom" I start the shower and get in "I never do!" I grab my dressing gown and wrap a towel around my head as I get out the shower and head back into the room and see a chair and table set up with loads of makeup set up and hair supplies "wow!" Roxy smirks and shrugs "it's your first dance so I want you to look the best there" I smirk and walk towards her "thank you!" She shrugs and nods towards the chair "now sit" I sit on the chair and she takes the towel of my head and dries my hair a little with it before reaching for the hair dryer and hair bobbles "let's begin" she plays the radio and smiles into the mirror at me before turning the hair dryer on and starts on my hair. After a few hours she steps back and takes a deep breath "I done good!" I roll my eyes and turn around towards the mirror "wow!" She walks towards me and smiles handing me my dress "your welcome" I take the dress and hug her "thank you." She looks at the dress and nods "you get changed and I will get shoes" I look towards my alarm clock still upside down "what time is it?" She looks at her watch and smiles "5PM" I shake my head and quickly walk towards my bed "Liam is going to be here in an hour" she rolls her eyes and walks towards the door "still got an hour don't worry." I get changed into the dress and try zip it up at the back as Roxy walks in "want help?" She laughs softly and I nod "yes please." She walks towards me and zips me up and hands me a pair of peach heels "these are my favourite pair so don't ruin them!" I nod and smirk "I won't." I sit on the bed and smile "drink?" She raises her eyebrow and shakes his head "ok but just one" I smirk and nod "yes!" I stand up and follow her out the room and downstairs "go in there and I will bring it in" she points towards the living room and I nod and smile "ok." I walk into the living room and place the heels on the sofa next to me and sit down gently. "Here" I look up and see Roxy holding out a glass "what is it?" She sits down sipping on hers "just try it" I take a small sip and shake my head "its sweet?" She nods and smirks "its gin" I look at it and lick my lips "I might need to borrow some" she shakes her head and laughs sarcastically "no!" I roll my eyes and point towards my mouth "some lipstick idiot" she laughs nervously and looks down "of course it's already in your bag" I raise my eyebrow and smirk "my bag?" She points towards the hooks behind the door "I got you a few things in case" I laugh nervously and shake my head "I'm worried to even look in it." Roxy walks towards the TV and sticks the radio on before heading into the kitchen "you want a beer?" I look towards the door and nod "ok sure!" She walks in holding 2 beers and hands me one "so you nervous?" I shrug and open the beer "no why would I be?" She opens hers and shrugs "because you are going with Liam and Brody isn't allowed to go? I thought you wanted to see where things with Brody were going?" I shrug and smirk "I do but I can see if Brody wants to come to Ryders afterparty" Roxy raises her eyebrows and smirks "after party?" I nod and smile "yeah?" She rolls her eyes and shakes her head "and why am I just hearing about this now?" I laugh nervously and shrug "I thought I mentioned it before" she stands up and walks towards the drawers and grabs something "no!" She gives me it and smiles "take this then" I look at the thing she sticks in my hand and shake my head "a whistle?" She nods firmly and sits back down "I know what teenage boys are like so if you need help then blow on it and it will get someone's attention" I roll my eyes and stick it in my bra "fine but only because it will make you feel better" she smirks and nods "thank you." I sip on the rest of my gin and as soon as I take my last sip Roxy stands up and takes my glass "another?" Before I could answer her she disappears into the kitchen "yeah why not!" I shake my head and smile leaning back into the sofa "I will get it!" I look behind me and shake my head "get what?" The doorbell goes as Roxy walks past smirking "that" I quickly sit up straight and look towards the door "hey you!" I see Liam Walk in and smile "wow!" I shake my head and blush "are haven't even seen my dress yet" he shrugs and smirks "you look amazing anyway" I stand up and turn around "thanks." I pick up my shoes and nod "ready?" He smiles and nods "yeah our ride awaits" I raise my eyebrow and shake my head nervously "what ride?" I walk towards him and he opens the door "this one." I look outside and see a white limo waiting outside "that's for us?" Roxy hands me my bag and laughs softly "it's all yours" I nod and smile "I love it!" I smile and hug Roxy "I will see you tomorrow" I stick my shoes on and Roxy laughs nervously "tomorrow?" I stand up straight and nod "yeah I told Ryder I would help clean up" I grab a bag from the hallway cupboard "don't worry I got clothes and stuff packed" I kiss her cheek and smile "see you tomorrow?" She nods and smiles "ok but make sure you text me every hour" I nod and walk out the door "on the house. I know" she nods and walks towards the door entrance and waves "have fun!" Ryder waves and smiles "I will take care of her Roxy don't worry" Roxy smirks and nods firmly "make sure you do!" Liam opens the limo door and I get inside and look around the limo and see a disco ball inside and a basket of ice and vodka with cans of cola "wow!" Liam gets in and closes the door behind him "Craig gave us these for me working so hard this week" he sticks my bag on the floor and smirks handing me a glass and pours vodka and cola into it "well done you!" He pours himself one and holds it up "too a good night?" I cheers him and smirk "too a good night." Liam rolls down the window and looks towards the drive "let's go" the car starts and I look out the window and wave towards Roxy and see Brody standing at his room window looking at me smiling softly. I smile and drink a sip of my vodka before closing the window and looking around "music?" I look at Liam and he reaches for a button on the top of the limo "yeah why not" he presses the button and smirks "I love this song!" He starts singing along to One Direction and I can't help but giggle "great voice" he smirks and leans back "I know" he continues to sing and I lean back and drink the rest of my vodka.

When the limo finally stops I look at Liam and nod "you ready?" He smirks and opens the door "are you?" I nod and he gets out and I follow. He holds his arm out so I wrap my arm around it and he smiles "let's do this then" he walks forward and I follow him into the school gym entrance. I spot Abbie and Shannon at the door arguing "you not like them?" I look at Liam and smile "it's the other way around actually." I look down and Liam gentle squeezes my arm "who needs them" I look at him and smirk "your cousin used to date on of them" he looks at me and shakes his head "what one?" I look up them and smirk "the one in the pink dress" he looks at her and shakes his head "my cousin dates terrible woman" I laugh softly and nod firmly "she is terrible." As we pass them Abbie looks over and scoffs "you actually showed?" I step forward and Liam holds his hand out "she's not worth it" Abbie looks at him and smirks "and she's not worth coming here with" she steps forward and winks at him "when you're done with her come find me." She looks him up and down and shrugs "I'm Abbie and you are?" He shakes his head and turns around "leaving this conversation" he walks towards the gym entrance and I follow him giggling under my breath. I walk in with my arm around Liam's and look around "this place looks not bad" Liam smirks and nods towards a table at the back "drink?" I nod and he lets go of my arm and smiles "I will be two tics." He walks towards the table and I watch him but spot Ryder in the back speaking too Ricky at the back of the gym 'I wonder why he isn't with Abbie?' He looks around and meets his eyes on me and smirks looking me up and down before handing his cup to Ricky and starts walking towards me. Liam walks over towards me at the same time and when Ryder spots him he stops and smiles softly before looking towards the floor shaking his head and walking back towards Ricky. "Here you go" Liam hands me the cup and winks "I added a little extra in" he shows me a small bottle of vodka inside his suit jacket "good I will need it." He looks around and smirks "why? Is that Abbie giving you bother again?" I look around and shake my head "no. I think she actually left" I look towards Ryder and nod "just don't think Ryder likes that I'm here with you." Liam looks towards Ryder and shakes his head "Ryder? We used to all play together when we was little" I raises my eyebrow and smirk "really?" He nods and smiles "yeah him and Brody was best friends until some girl came along" I laugh nervously and nod "that would be Abbie" Liam laughs sarcastically "your joking?" I shake my head and smile "nope" he looks towards Ryder and shakes his head "I'm going over" I grab his arm and shake my head "play nice" he looks at me and nods "I always do" he walks over and I take a large sip of my drink and follow him over. Ryder looks at us and stands up straight with a serious look on his face as we approach "hi" he looks at me and nods "hey" I smile and look down nervously "hi." 'Why is this so awkward?' I look up and see Ryder smirking "how have you been?" He looks at Liam and leans forward holding his hand out "yeah I've been good. How you been keeping?" I roll my eyes and drink the rest of my drink finishing it "I'm going to get another drink." I walk towards the drink table and Ricky runs after me "Amy!" I turn around and he smiles looking at my head "you covered that scar good" I laugh nervously and shake my head "yeah Roxy did it." He walks towards the drink table and smiles "what you drinking?" I look around and smile "lemonade" he goes into his pocket and pulls out a small flash "vodka?" I look around and nod "I think I will need it" I look towards Liam and Ryder laughing as Ricky pours some vodka into my lemonade. He smiles and nods towards the photo area "shall we get a picture and make good memories?" I look over and smirk "I would love too." He walks over and I follow behind him fixing my hair before standing in front of the large white screen with a camera "ready?" I look towards the cameraman and nod "yeah." He holds with camera up and smiles "say sausages" I laugh softly and smile "sausages!" The flash goes off and the cameraman nods "perfect" I shake my head and close my eyes "wow that flash is bright" Ricky laughs softly and nods "I agree my eyes are still burning." I spot a photo booth and smile "we should get Ryder and Liam and all get a group picture" he looks towards them and smirks "I will get them and you stay here" he walks towards them and I nod "ok." I walk towards the photo booth and sit down "get up!" I look out and see Abbie and Shannon "what?" She rolls her eyes and shrugs "get out" I laugh sarcastically and cross my arms "no." She steps forward as Liam grabs her arm "leave" she looks at him and smirks "any excuse to touch me" she rubs his arm and he smirks and shakes his head "leave" he pulls his arm away from her and looks at me "you ok?" I stand up and smile "nothing I can't handle" he cuddles me and smiles "good." He looks at the photo booth and smirks "so we getting a picture of just us before Ryder and Ricky come out the bathroom?" I look around and nod "yeah ok then." I walk towards the photo booth and sit down "come on" I tap the seat next to me and Liam smirks and walks in "ok what settings do you want?" He leans forward and points towards a wooden area "that because that's where you was heading the first time we met" I click on it and smile "good choice." I sit back and look at the screen '3 2 1' I smile as the flash goes off and look at the screen and see '3 2 1' come up again so I quickly grab Liam and hold his head next to mine and pull a funny face "you want to take they kind of pictures?" I laugh softly and nod "funny pictures are the best" he looks at the screen and nods "ok well what about this" he holds my nose up and does a rabbit ear sign above my head and I look towards the screen and smile as the flash goes of "thank you" I smile and nod "that's it done then." The machine starts printing and I see a strip of photos come down "I will get these copied and give you it tomorrow?" He smiles and nods "ok" I stick the pictures in my bag and follow him out the photo booth as Ryder and Ricky walk over "group picture?" I smile and nod "yes!" I walk towards the man holding the camera and smile "can you do a picture for 4?" He looks at Ricky, Ryder and Liam and nod "sure" I smirk and look at them "come on" they follow me too the white screen and we all go into a pose "ready?" I nod and smile "ok say cheese" I smile softly as the flash goes off on the camera. "Done" I close my eyes and shake my head "I won't get used to that flash" I walk towards the photobooth and smile "let's go here next" they follow me towards it and Ricky shakes his head "I'm good. I'm going to get a drink" Liam looks at me and smirks "me too" he nods towards my drink and shrugs "you want one?" I nod and smile softy "yes please" they walk away and Ryder opens the curtain for the photo booth "just us two then?" I smile and nod "looks like it" I walk into the booth and sit down and Ryder sits beside me pressing the button. '3 2 1' I smile as the flash goes off and look at Ryder and see her rubbing his eyes "my god that's bright" I smirk and nod "another 2 to go." I look back at the screen and nod "ready?" He look at the screen and nods '3 2 1' I look at Ryder and pull a funny face "so one more?" I nod and smile "yeah." He looks at the screen and smirks "close your eyes" I raise my eyebrows and smirk "what?" He closes his eyes and nods "like an unexpected picture" I shrug and smile "ok?" I look at the screen and see '3' I close my eyes and feel hands touch my face and turn my head around towards Ryder so I open my eyes and he kisses me as the flash goes off. I shake my head in shock and laugh nervously "what was that?" He looks at the pictures and smile "sorry I just always wanted to do that." I look at the picture and smirk "you can keep that one" I stand up and walk out the booth and see Ricky and Liam walking over "we will talk about this later" Ryder walks towards my side and smirks "you didn't like it?" I roll my eyes and sigh "just don't say anything." Liam and Ricky approach us smiling "here you go" Liam hands me a glass and I smile "thank you." Ricky looks at Ryder and nods towards the fire exit "want to go out for a smoke?" Ryder looks at me and I look down nervously "sure!" They head towards the fire exit and I look up as they walk away "you still got any" I look at Liam and smirk "anything stronger?" He nods and holds his hand out and I give him my cup and he pours some vodka into it before giving me it back "thanks." I take a long sip of it and sigh "better." He laughs softly and shakes his head "let's get a photo" I look towards the camera man and nod "ok." I follow him towards the camera man and he holds his arm around my waist pulling me towards him "what a lovely couple" he holds his camera up and smirks "now smile" I look at Liam and laugh softly shaking my head before turning towards the camera man and smiling. The flash goes off and this time doesn't hurt as much, I was getting used to it. Liam rubs his eyes and shakes his head "no more pictures" I laugh softly and shake my head "I'm used to It now" he smirks and looks back towards the camera man "so we are a lovely couple apparently" he looks down and shakes his head "you wish" Liam looks at me and smirks "maybe if my cousin wasn't so hung up on you." I roll my eyes and wrap my arm around his "he isn't!" I drag him towards the dance floor and smile "want to dance?" He holds his hand out and I place mine perfectly into his warm hand "your cold?" I shake my head and smile "I'm fine" he takes his suit jacket of and wraps it around me "here" I smile softly and place my hands back into his and we continue to dance. After 4 songs I stop and sigh "my feet are sore now" he looks down at my heels and laughs sarcastically "I don't blame them" he wraps his arm around me "put your weight on me and we can go sit down" he nods towards the tables at the fire exit and I nod "ok" I wrap my arm around his and stick some weight onto him and follow him towards the tables and sit down. Ricky and Ryder walk over and smile "we are heading to mine in 10 if youse want to head up with us?" I look at Liam and smile "we have a limo but we will follow youse?" Ryder nods and smirks "ok." He walks towards a group of boys at another table and starts speaking to them "you want help?" I shake my head and smile "huh?" He looks towards my feet and smiles "you manage to walk in those?" I smirk and nod "yeah I should be fine plus I got other shoes in my bag back in the limo" Liam nods firmly and smirks. I look over towards Ryder and see him waving towards the boys before heading towards us "ready?" Liam looks towards them and nods "yeah" he stands up holding his hand out so I stand up and take his hand and wrap my arm around his. "We are heading now" I nod at Ryder and smile "ok well we will be right behind you just send us the address" Ryder nods and smiles "ok" he looks at Ricky and nods "let's go" they walk towards the exit and we follow. Ryder nods towards the limo "that yours?" I nod and smile "ok well I will tell the driver the address" I smile and nod before getting into the limo and take my heels of "can you give me that bag please?" He hands me my bag and I go into it and grab a pair of trainers and socks out "thank you" I stick the heels into it and hand him it back and he sticks it back onto the seat. I stick my socks and shoes on before grabbing a bottle from the bucket of ice "wine? Fancy" I open the wine and drink it from the bottle "you not want a glass?" I shake my head and sigh "no this is good." Liam nods towards his jacket and smirks "hand me the vodka" I go into the pocket and hand him the bottle of vodka before drinking the rest of the wine. "What you nervous about?" I shrug and look down "what do you mean?" He leans forward and takes the empty bottle of wine "you have drank a full bottle in 10 minutes" he raises his eyebrows and smirks "want to talk about it?" I lean back and shake my head "just never been to a party" he laughs sarcastically "really?" I smile softly and nod firmly "yeah." He pulls the sofa up and reveals a mini fridge "here" he hands me a bottle of whiskey and smirks "don't want you being twitchy all night so have some of this and it should relax you." I take the bottle and open it taking a sip "it's disgusting!" I lick my lips repeatedly "try it with this" he hands me a can of cola and a glass "thanks." I pour some whiskey into the class and a dash of coke "it's actually meant to be coke with a dash of whiskey but that's" he shakes his head and leans back "you do what you feel is best" I smirk and look at the glass before downing it in one. "That better?" I nod and smile "a little" he holds his hand out and smiles "let me try" I hand him the whiskey and he takes a sip and shakes his head "god that is horrible" he wipes his mouth and sighs "told ya!" I take the bottle back and pour another cola and whiskey and down it. The limo stops and I look towards the window "are we here?" Liam rolls the window down and nods "guess so?" I spot Ricky at the top of the stairs and smile "yeah there's Ricky!" I grab my bags and open the door "I will take this" I grab the whiskey and stick it in my bag before heading up the stairs towards Ricky. "Hey!" He turns around and I see him on the phone "youse finally made it?" I smile and nod "yeah" he gets of the phone and nods towards the front door "just head in and help yourself too whatever" I look inside and shrug "where's Ryder?" He rings someone else and smirks "inside getting changed" I nod firmly and look at Liam "ready?" He smiles softly and nods so I open the front door and head in. I look around the modern decorated house with a wooden staircase and nod firmly "wow!" Liam smiles and looks around "I haven't been here in years" I look at Liam as he looks around examining everything "you have been here?" He looks at me and nods "when we was little we used to come here every summer and go fishing at the lake out back and spend most of our times in the pool" I raise my eyebrow and smirk "pool?" He nods and points towards the back of the house "there's a pool in the back yard" I shake my head and scoff "of course there is!" I nod and take a deep breath "let's get a drink then" I walk forward and Liam shakes his head and laughs softly "wrong way to the kitchen" I look around and point towards another door "there?" He nods and smirks "yeah" I walk into the room and smile "thanks" he follows he and walks towards the cupboard like it was his house and grabs two glasses handing me one "thanks." I pour some whiskey into the glass and he walks towards the fridge and grabs a can of cola before handing me it "you want one?" He shakes his head and grabs his vodka "I will stick to something nice thanks." I shrug and hold the whiskey up "suit yourself" I down it in one and shake my head "so you want to give me a tour?" The back door opens and a bunch of people walk in "maybe later" I nod and smile "ok." Ryder walks in and waves at me "hey you!" I wave and smile "hi" he hold a remote up and presses a button on it before sticking it in his jacket pocket "let's get this party started!" Music starts playing and the crowd of people who walked in start cheering. Liam looks around and smiles softly "what?" He nods behind me and blushes "a girl I kissed one summer just walked in" I turn around and see a tall tanned girl with long shiny ginger hair "what are you still standing here for then? Go over there and say hi" he looks at me and smiles "you don't mind" I roll my eyes and shove him softly "no! Now get out of here you loser" he laughs nervously and nods "ok I will come find you after ok?" I smile softly and nod "ok" he walks towards the girl. I look around and spot Ryder speaking to a tanned muscular boy wearing just shorts "wow!" I shake my head and look down blushing 'did I just say that out loud?' I look up and see him looking towards me smirking 'another whiskey Amy, another whiskey!' I grab the whiskey and down most of the bottle before heading towards the back door 'I guess I will give myself a tour.' I look outside and see a large pool with people already in it with their dresses and suits on 'not drunk enough.' I shake my head and walk back inside banging into the man Ryder was speaking too "sorry" he looks up and smirks "not that sorry." I blush and shake my head "what?" He shrugs and holds his hand out "bumping into you is a good ice breaker" I shake his head and he holds it and kisses it "Joe" I laugh nervously and blush "Amy." He holds a beer out and smiles "beer?" I shrug and take it "thanks" he holds his finger up and nods "two seconds" he heads back inside and comes out a few seconds after holding another beer and a bottle of vodka with two shot glasses "come on." He walks towards the back of the pool and opens a gate "am I going too trip over or something?" he shakes his head and smirks "no you should be fine" I walk through the fence look around "what is this?" He reaches down and presses a button on the ground and floor lights appear along a pathway and ends at a double bed swing "you didn't bring me here too" I raise my eyebrow and nod towards the bed "what? God no!" He laughs sarcastically and shakes his head "I'm not like that." He walks towards the bed and sits down "I just find it nice and peaceful out here" I smile and walk towards him and sit down "it will probably look better in the day?" He nods firmly and smiles "true" I look swing the bed to the side and he smirks "let's get you back inside before Ryder sends a search party" he stands up and I follow "what? Why would he do that?" He looks at me and raises his eyebrow and shakes his head "let's go" he fast walks towards the house and I shake my head and try catch up "Joe wait!" He disappears into the crowd and into the house "dammit!" I look around but no sign on him but I spot Ryder speaking to a group of boys all doing shops "I guess I will see what he says about it' I smirk and towards Ryder as he finishes his shot. He shakes his head and wipes his mouth "hey" he hands me a shot glass and I shrug and take it "why not" a boy holding a shot bottle pours my glass and Ryder nods "3 2 1" he downs the shot and I down mine and smirk "that's surprisingly nice" he shakes his head and licks his lips "really?" I laugh softly and nod "yeah." He looks around and smiles "come on and I will introduce you to some people" Ryder takes his hand and walks towards a crowd of people talking by on the sofa "hey guys!" They all look at Ryder and wave "this is Amy" they all look at me and I smile nervously "hey." A girl in an orange skin-tight dress stands up and holds her hand out "I'm Cheryl" I shake her hand and smile "nice to meet you." She looks at Ryder and smirks "I will take care of her" she looks towards the stairs and nods "you go handle that!" Ryder turns around and shakes his head "not the hamster guys come on!" I turn around and see a boy holding a hamster in his hand stroking it "I will come find you after ok?" I smile and nod "ok" he walks towards them and takes the hamster of him before heading upstairs with it. I look at Cheryl and smile "want a beer?" She nods and follows me into the kitchen "sounds good." She grabs two beers and opens them with her teeth before handing me one "so how do you know Ryder?" I smile and take a sip "we go to school together" she nods firmly and smiles "so you're the new girl he was talking about?" I look down towards the floor blushing and shake my head "he talks about me?" She takes a sip and shrugs "he did in his dream one time." I smirk and look towards the stairs "so how do you know Ryder?" She looks towards the wall before me and nods "I'm his little sisters' best friend" I look behind me towards the canvas photo of Ryder and Chloe on the wall and smirk "Chloe?" She nods and smiles "you know her?" I shrug and laugh softly "I met her once when she was with Ryder in the mall." She looks towards the canvas and smirks "she's awesome. You will love her" she walks towards the back door and looks outside "is she coming?" I walk towards her and she nods firmly and smiles "she's at her boyfriend's right now but Ryder thinks she's at our other friends so if he asks then go with that but she is going to pop back about" she looks at her watch and nods "about an hour she said." I look at the clock and smirk "is it 11PM already?!" I drink most of my beer and smile "Ryders music taste is horrible" Cheryl laughs softly and shakes her head "it's the DJ's" I look around and shrug "DJ?" She nods and smiles "well I'm going to find this DJ and request a song" she drinks her beer in one and sticks it on the table before grabbing another "I will come with you" I walk towards the living room and she follows me. I look around and Cheryl points towards the back of the house "there!" I look over and see a boy sitting behind a table with two large speakers and a laptop in front of him "come on!" I walk towards him and he looks up and smirks "hello ladies" Cheryl rolls her eyes and sits on the side of the table "change the songs they are rubbish" he looks at me and smirks "do youse want anything particular on?" Cheryl looks at me and smirks "try this" he hands him a disc and he shrugs "alright then but Ryder asks I am sending him your way" I roll my eyes and smirk "Ryder won't say anything its ok." He shrugs and sticks the disk in "alright then" I smirk and walk towards the kitchen drinking the rest of my beer and sticking it in the bin and grab a bottle of whiskey "this party needs a little bit more fun!" Cheryl laughs softly and nods "I like you're thinking" she grabs two whiskey glasses and I pour whiskey into them and she hands me one "to new friends?" I hold my glass up and she smirks and nods "cheers too that!" She cheers my glass and I smile and down the whiskey in one "god I hate whiskey" Cheryl shakes her head and licks her lips "I like it" she raises her eyebrow and looks at me "really?" I smirk and nod "yeah." She sticks the glass down and shrugs "all yours then" I smile and stick the glass down and pick the bottle up "come on let's go mingle." Cheryl walks into the living room and I follow "hey you!" I see the hands wrap around Cheryl's waist picking her up "Deano!" She hugs him and kisses him on the lips "you made it!" He sticks her down and she shakes her head "Deano this is my friend Amy" she looks at me and smiles softly "Amy this is my boyfriend Deano" he holds his hand out and I place mine in it to shake it "nice to meet you" he pulls my hand towards his mouth and kisses it, pressing his warm soft lips on the back of my hand. "Isn't he a gentleman?" He looks right into my eyes and smiles flirty "yeah" I move my hand away and Cheryl wraps her arm around his "I will catch up with you later?" I smile softly and nod firmly "yeah ok" Deano smirks at me and grabs the bottle of whiskey from me before getting pulled towards the back door by Cheryl. I smile softly and grab another bottle of whiskey before heading into the living room, I spot Liam by the front door kissing the girl from earlier and I smile and nod 'get in there Liam!' I look down and shake my head 'I should probably not just stand here and stare' I look up and spot Joe leaning against the wall looking at me smiling before waving "hi!" I shake my head and walk towards him "what you doing here standing yourself?" he shrugs and takes the whiskey out my hand and takes a sip "I was waiting for you" he touches my face and I shake my head and pull away "your drunk?" He shrugs and hands me the whiskey back "that's disgusting" I roll my eyes and take a sip "why does no one like whiskey in this town?" He shrugs and pulls a flask out from his jacket pocket "want some?" I look at it and smile nervously "what is it?" He winks and hands me it "something nicer than that." I shrug and take a drink of it, as it runs through my throat I taste a burning feeling as I gulp it "wow!" I look at it and smile "that's got a weird after kick" I hand him it back and smile "so what is it?" He holds his finger towards his mouth and smiles "my secret recipe." I roll my eyes and take the flack of him and run away "oi!" I look behind me and see him standing up straight before trying to run after me "don't drink all of that!" I run out the back garden and close the door behind me looking at him through the glass door smirking before downing the rest of it in one "Amy no!" I finish it and wipe my mouth "oops" I open the door and hand him it back "now you need to give me the recipe so I can help you make more." He sticks the flask upside down and nothing comes out "no you don't understand Amy" he looks at me and shakes his head "there was" he looks behind me and shakes his head "never mine" he grabs a bottle of water and hands me it "take this" I hold it and shake my head "what?" He looks behind me again before taking a deep breath "I got to go!" He walks out the back door and disappears "weird" I shake my head and turn around and see Liam and that girl walk towards me "hey you!" I wave and Liam looks at me and smile "hi" he walks towards me with the girl he was with earlier and waves "this is Kim" I look at her and smile softly "Kim this is Amy" I hold my hand out and she shakes her head and smiles before going in for a hug "please! We are all friends here" I cuddle her and she smiles "I'm going to go catch up with Julie but I will come find you after ok?" Liam nods and smiles "ok" she kisses his cheek before running of into the living room. "Having fun?" He looks at me and smiles "yeah you?" He looks at the bottle in my hand and I shake my head "yeah." He takes the whiskey and looks at the tiny bit left "how much have you had?" I shrug and lean against the table "this and a few beers" I look at the water beside me and nod "and some drink that Joe made up." Liam raises his eyebrow and smirks "Joe?" I shrug and smile "he is a friend of Ryders" he nods firmly and laughs nervously "Joe Skinner?" I shrug and grab the bottle of water as my stomach starts too feel funny "I don't know his second name." He points towards the bottle of water and sighs "and he gave you this after he gave you some?" I laugh nervously and look towards the ground "I actually stole it of him and drank it all" I shake my head and sigh "then he acted all worried and handed me this" I look at Liam and shake my head "why?" Liam has a concerned look in his eyes as he looks me up and down "how do you feel?" I rub my stomach and smile "I think the whiskey is getting to me but don't worry" I grab a bottle of cider and smile "this will help." He takes the cider of me and hands me the bottle of water "let's go." I shake my head and step back "what? Where?" He grabs another bottle of water and wraps his arm around mine "home!" I shake my head and move my arm away "what? No!" I look towards the back door and smile as I spot Joe and Ryder "there is Joe now so go ask him what was in the drink before you start going all crazy" Liam looks outside and spots Joe "I am going to kill him!" He lets go of my arm and I try grab him but I lose my strength and his arm pulls through my fingers and he storms out the back yard towards Joe and Ryder. I walk towards the back door but stop when my stomach hurts more and shake my head "move!" I run towards the living room and upstairs 'please let no one be in the bathroom!' I look around and sigh "where is the bathroom?" A girl points towards a door and smiles "thank you!" I run towards the door and try open it "typical!" The door is locked so I look around and run towards a room at the bottom of the hallway and open the door "come on!" I look around and see a bedroom with 3 doors "please let one of these be a toilet!" I run towards the door at the back and open it and see a cupboard full of shoes "oh come on!" I run towards the other door and open it and smirk as I see a toilet "yes!" I run in closing the door behind me and run towards the toilet pan lifting the toilet seat up and pull my hair to the side as I begin to throw up. I wipe my mouth after I finish and walk towards the sink washing my hands and mouth "good job I brought my lipstick" I smirk and reach into the bag and grab my lipstick before applying it to my lips. I grab a chewing gum and chew it before heading towards the bathroom door "no stop!" I reach for the handle but stop when I hear someone in the other end of the door "get of me!" I shake my head and open the door and see

Kim lying on the bed with someone on top of her pinning her hands down "Liam?" The figure turns around and I shake my head in disbelief "Deano?" I run towards him and shove him of Kim "get of her you weirdo!" Kim manages to get free "run!" She looks at me and shakes her head before running out the room "you can't treat girls like that!" I turn around and face Deano and see an evil look in his eyes before seeing his fist come towards my face and knocking me out unconscious. When I come back around I look around and realise I was in the bedroom ensuite bathroom but I mange too look out the door and I see Deano pacing up and down the room speaking too someone. I look towards the door and see another shadow "what will I do?" I look at the other figure and try make them out but they look towards me and shakes their head "she is awake!" They walks out the door and sighs "give her some more powder" I look around panicking and spot my bag on the floor 'the whistle!' I reach for my bag and open it reaching inside for the whistle Roxy packed me before blowing into it the hardest I can. Deano runs towards me and grabs the whistle out my hand before punching me and standing on my leg "you stupid bitch!" He runs towards the door and takes a deep breath "this isn't over." He runs out the door leaving me lying on the bathroom floor with my leg in agony and blood all over my face 'stay awake!' I shake my head to try keep my eyes open as I feel them start to close "hello?!" I look towards the door and see Kim looking towards me "she's in here!" She stops at the door and I see Liam running towards me "Brody!" As I feel my eyes drift of I see Brody walk into the bathroom and wrap his arm around my neck lifting me into his warm strong arms "Amy? It's going to be ok" I look at him and speak in shock "Brody?" He smiles softly and shakes his head carrying me out the bathroom "shh its ok" I look at him and smile before my eyes finally give in and I go unconscious again. I wake up in my own bed and see my room door wide open "Roxy" I sit up and look around "Roxy?!" I get up and see Roxy run into my room "Amy!" She runs towards me and grabs my tightly for a cuddle "thank god you are ok!" I laugh nervously and hug her "what happened?" She sits on the bed and I sit next to her rubbing my head "you don't remember?" I look towards my window and shake my head "did Brody have to carry me home?" She nods and smiles "yeah you was pretty wasted" I laugh nervously as some of last night comes back to me 'oh my god! I was attacked by that Deano.' I jump up and grab jeans and a top and run out the door "I'm going Brody's!" I grab my shoes and jacket and run towards the door opening it "hey!" I see Joe standing outside "hi" he smiles softly and nods "are you ok?" I look down and nod "I'm not sure" I look at him and smile "I'm trying to figure out what happened last night." He raises his eyebrow and smirks "you don't remember?" I shake my head and laugh nervously "no." He nods firmly and looks towards a car behind him "let's go for lunch and I can try fill you in?" I nod and close the door behind me "sure why not" I follow him towards the car and get in. He drives to a diner and smiles "this is my favourite place" he gets out the car and I follow him towards the diner door. A woman walks towards us smiling "table for 2?" Joe nods and smiles "yes please" the woman walks towards a table and places 2 menus down "can I get youse something to drink?" I sit down and smile "can I have a cola please?" She nods and looks at Joe "and for you sir?" Joe looks at me and smiles "I will have a cola too please" she nods and walks away. I look at the menu and sigh "so how bad did I end up last night?" Joe laughs nervously and shakes his head "you passed out in the bathroom and Liam called his cousin and he came and took you home" I look at him and shrug "I remember Deano trying to attack Kim before turning on me." Joe coughs and raises his eyebrows "really?" I nod and smile "I hope she's ok and for Deano's sake he best stay out my way" Joe smiles and looks at his menu "so you going to tell Ryder about Deano?" I shake my head and sigh "no because I'm sure he was just drunk but if I see him I will be telling him what he done!" Joe smile and shakes his head "that a brave thing to do" I shrug and take a deep breath "I just want to move on from it." The waitress comes back and smiles "are youse ready to order?" I nod and smile "yes please."

After lunch Joe grabs the check and sticks money down "not fast your last" I shake my head and laugh softly before sticking 10 down "a tip" he raises his eyebrow and smirks "you can come to my work and tip me that if you want." I smile and stand up "where do you work?" He stands up and grabs his jacket "Omar's" I smile and look him up and down "the bar in town?" He smirks and looks down nodding his head "yeah" I raise my eyebrows and sigh "how old are you?" He rolls his eyes and walks towards the door "how old do you think I am?" I follow him out and shrug "didn't think about it but about 20?" He smiles and nods "21 so close enough." I get into his car and he hands me a note "since I didn't give you my number last night" I smile softly a stick it in my pocket "call me when you want to go for dinner" I laugh nervously and nod "next Saturday works for me?" He smiles and nods "I'm working next Saturday at 8 but we could go before? I can pick you up at 6 and you could even come and see me work? Get a friend too meet you there?" I smirk and nod "ok" I laugh nervously and shake my head "I can't I'm not old enough and I don't have fake ID" Joe smirks and winks "leave that with me. Just tell your friend to say my name at the door and they will get in" I smirk and nod "ok thank you." He pulls up outside my house and I sigh "so I guess I will see you Saturday?" He smirks and holds his hand out so I place my hand in his and he kisses it "can't wait!" I get out the car and wave before running towards my house and open the door. "Amy is that you?!" I look upstairs and smile "yeah it's me!" I walk into the kitchen and Roxy runs down "did Brody fill in the missing pieces?" I look down towards the floor and laugh nervously "I actually went for lunch with Joe" she raises her eyebrows and smirks "and who is Joe?" I walk towards the fridge and grab a bottle of water "a boy I met last night." I close the fridge and smile "so Brody is out the picture?" I roll my eyes and take a sip of the water "can't a girl and boy be friends without anything happening?" She smiles and nods firmly "sorry. Of course they can" I smile and walk towards the back door "good but I am going out with him for dinner Saturday" she shakes her head and sighs "so Brody is out the picture?" I shrug and smile "I don't know yet" I look towards Brody's house and smile softly "we haven't had that conversation and I still don't think he likes me like that!" Roxy smirks and shakes her head "believe me! He does" She look towards Bear and smile "I'm taking Bear out" I look towards her and smile "ok well I'm going back to bed" I yawn and grab my bottle of water and head upstairs and grab a long t-shirt before sitting on the side of my bed and change before getting under the covers and falling asleep.

I wake up a few hours later and look at my alarm clock "3AM?!" I sit up and see a slice of pizza on a plate on my bedside cabinet "can't believe I slept for so long" I look at the pizza and shake my head before sticking it in the bin and head downstairs. I look in the fridge and grab the milk and make cereal "why does this always taste better at night?" I smirk and walk towards the window and look towards the patch of grass where the secret room is and smile "why not." I stick my cereal on the table before heading into the hallway and grab my bag and head out the back yard. I walk towards the door entrance and open it and head down the ladder closing it behind me and turn the lights on. "Where did I leave of last time?" I spot the file from the drawer lying by the CCTV so I walk towards it turning on the CCTV and sitting down opening the folder. "File number 4 The Secret powers of Kalispell" I laugh softly and shake my head "gets me every time" I flip the page and read another file "File 8 Hero's or Villains?" I shake my head and read it "Are the people with the powers among us evil or good? Should be let them have the chance to explain if they are? The answer is no! If they have powers they can turn and destroy all mankind. We believe that with they have a weakness and this should be used against them for our safety and the safety of our kids and their future." I close the book and lean back "these people are crazy" I smile and look around "what else is down here then?" I open my bag and go into the envelope and look at the map "another door?" I look around and smile "there!" I stand up and walk towards a wall with a bookshelf and look back at the map "Romeo and Juliet" I look at the bookshelf and spot the book so I pull it and the bookshelf moves and I look behind it and see a large narrow tunnel "so this leads into the living room!" I smirk and nod "cool." I close the bookshelf and look back towards the map and spot a question Craig on the map in the cupboard Roxy is using as her closet "what is that?" I look towards the CCTV and see Roxy still sleeping "should probably check it out tomorrow." I head towards the ladder and shake my head "give me something to read when I can't sleep" I grab the folder and press the button and head back up the ladder and into the house. I grab a bottle of water and stick the folder in my bedside drawer before heading into bed. I toss and turn a few times before finally sitting back up and checking the time "5AM!" I take a deep breath and nod "why not" I grab the folder and start reading it but after a few hours I yawn and drift off to sleep with the folder lying next to me.

The next morning I wake up and look towards my alarm clock "9AM? I slept for pretty much a full day!" I get out of bed and quickly get dressed before heading downstairs. "Morning!" I see Roxy in the kitchen "why are you not at work?" She looks at the clock and smiles "I don't start till 9" I look at the clock and smirk "its" I look at my watch and show her "9:10?" She looks at her phone and laughs nervously "I got too got!" She runs out the door grabbing her jacket and keys "bye!" I wave and smile as she closes the door behind her. I look towards the back yard and see Liam outside playing with Bella "bear?" I look towards Bear and smirk "come on boy." I open the back door and Bear runs out and barks towards the fence making Liam look over and smile "hey!" He waves and I wave as he walks towards the fence picking up Bella and jumping over the fence before sticking her down. "How you feeling?" I smile and shrug "ok" he looks towards Brody's house and sighs "do you remember anything?" I smile softly and shake my head "no" he nods towards the grass behind him and smirks "want me to fill you in?" I smile and nod "ok." I walk towards the grass with him and sit down as the dogs run around playing together "so what do you remember?" I laugh nervously and shake my head "nothing really" he looks down and takes a deep breath "Kim went upstairs after she seen you run up and followed you into a room but she said that someone grabbed her and pinned her on the bed and started kissing her" he looks at me and smiles "then that's when she seen you walk out the bathroom and run towards her helping her get him of her." He laughs softly and nods "she said that you told her to run while you tried to pin him down?" I smile softly and shrug "is she ok?" He nods and smiles "thanks to you." I shrug and look towards Bear "I know that Brody took me home?" Liam nods and smiles "I called him after you told me that you drank Joe's drink and he showed up just in time by sounds of it" I laugh nervously and look towards Brody's house "that drink was nasty! It made me throw up" he laughs nervously and looks down. "Kim is coming over today so if you're not busy I'm sure she will like to thank you herself?" I smile and nod "she doesn't have too." He nods and stands up "I know but she will want too" I smile and stand up "ok well I will be in all day anyway." Liam looks towards Brody's house and sighs "I should go" I follow his eyes and see Brody standing by his back door "is he angry at me?" Liam looks at me and smiles softly "I don't know" he looks at Bella and whistles "he won't speak about it." He picks Bella up before heading towards the fence and climbing over it "I will see you later?" I smile and nod "ok" I wave as he walks towards Brody and they both walk into the house closing the door behind them. I sigh and turn around "what is his problem?" I head inside and grab Bears food bowl and give him some dog food before heading into the living room and turning on the TV. I turn the news on and grab my phone I scroll through my social media account and click on a news article when I see a picture of Roxy's ex Nathan "Nathan Smith 24 was arrested last night at 9:15PM when he was caught in the middle of a bar fight including another two men who have also been arrested. Mr Smith has just recently been let out of prison 2 weeks ago where he was inside for attempted murder on his ex-partner Miss Roxy Cole" I shake my head and lock my phone sticking it down "this is all Roxy needs!" I look towards the TV and stick on some cartoons before lying down and watching them for the rest of the afternoon.

The rest of the week flies by and as much as I enjoyed not getting up at 7AM I missed school and I missed having an excuse to see Brody every day. Every night I walked towards my window and looked through his and seen him with a girl every night for the week which bothered me more because I grew to like him and even though I didn't believe he liked me a bit of my wanted what everyone was saying was true but the proof was standing right in front of me when he walked towards the window and smirked towards me before closing his curtains. I take a deep breath trying to hold my anger and jealousy in and close my curtains "who does he think he is?!" I walk towards my bed and lie down under the covers tossing and turning before getting back up and heading downstairs into the kitchen. I grab a glass an get the milk from the fridge and pour myself a cold glass of it before walking towards the kitchen window and see Jennifer outside crying so I run out towards her and wave "you ok?" She smiles softly and wipes her tears away "just boys" I laugh softly and nod "jerks aren't they!" I look towards Brody's room and her eyes follow "don't worry about her" I look at her and laugh nervously "who?" She walks towards the fence and smiles "she's just a distraction because he found out that you have a date Saturday" I look towards his room widow and smile "really? If he wants my attention then that's the wrong way of getting it" she smiles softly and shrugs "boy ehh!" I nod and smile "I know" I take a deep breath and shrug "I hope whoever made you cry tonight has the worst life" she cleans her eyes and laughs softly "me too!" She looks towards Brody's room and sighs "tell him how you feel" I look towards his room window and shrug "I can't" I look down and shake my head "in case he doesn't feel the same?" I look at her and nod firmly "yeah" she shakes her head and smirks "he would be silly not too." She heads back towards the door and smiles "I'm having people over tomorrow night for my birthday if your date is really bad then you can come over or come over when you get back?" I smile softly and nod "I would love too." She heads back inside closing the door behind her and I look at Brody's room window before heading inside, I walk towards the fridge and grab a bottle of water before heading upstairs and towards the window and open it "hey!" I jump and look over towards Brody's room and see him hanging out the window smiling "hi" I smile softly and wave "you ok?" I shrug and laugh nervously "why wouldn't I be?" I lean out the window and raise my eyebrows "just making sure." He gives me flirty eyes making my stomach turn, he had a way to get me smiling and blushing and he knew it and he loved it. His smile disappears and he looks behind him "I got to go" I follow his eyes and see the girl standing up in Brody's jersey "yeah me too!" I close the curtains and head into bed 'how dare he!' I look towards the window and sigh "I will not let you get to me anymore Brody James!" I turn my light of and close my eyes drifting off to sleep.

I wake up the next morning feeling amazing "today is going to be a good day!" I grab clothes and place them on my bed before heading into the bathroom and turning the shower on. Roxy walks into my bedroom as I come out the shower and looks around "Amy?!" I head into the bedroom and smile "what?" She hands me a gift bag and smiles "a gift from me and Jeremy for your date tonight" I roll my eyes and take the bag "it's not a date but thank you." I look inside the bag and pull out a red skater dress "I love it" she heads out the room and smiles "so Jennifer is having a party tonight and Jeremy has asked if I will go and supervise with him" I laugh softly and shake my head "supervise? Jennifer is the most responsible teenage I know" Roxy shrugs and smiles "it's not her Jeremy is worried about" she looks towards Brody's room and I follow her eyes and see Brody through the window looking at us before closing his curtains "why what's Brody got to do with it?" Roxy smiles softly and looks down "I should go" she walks out the room and runs downstairs and out the door. I roll my eyes and dry my hair before grabbing my phone and start texting Joe "Hey Joe I got plans for after dinner so can't stay out to late but I would love to come and see you work for an hour and have a drink before dealing with this party after?" I send the message and look towards the clock "3PM" I look around and sigh "I'm sure Roxy won't mind be taking one beer?" I smirk and head downstairs and grab a beer from the hallway cupboard before heading into the living room and turn the TV on. After a few minutes the front door goes making me jump and spill the beer down my top "no!" I try rub it but makes it worse so I grab the blanket and wrap it around me and head towards the door and open it. I see Liam standing outside smiling "hey" I smile and open the door winder "hi" he nods towards the kitchen and shrugs "Roxy said that it was ok for me to take Bear out?" I look towards the kitchen and see Bear sitting by the door "come here boy!" He runs towards us and I grab his lead "where you taking him?" He looks behind him and I see Kim holding Bella "just for a hike." I nod firmly and smile "have fun" he smiles and walks down the stairs "will I be seeing you at Jen's party?" I smile and shrug "maybe" I close the door and head back into the living room turning the TV of and drink the rest of my beer. I look at the time and sigh "4PM" I head upstairs and grab my dress placing it neatly on the bed "guess I should get ready" I grab my hairbrush and start brushing my hair. Once I finish getting ready I look towards the clock and smile "5:55? Just in time." I look at my phone and see a new message from Joe "Means more time with just you so perfect. See you at 6 x" I smirk and run downstairs grabbing Roxy's heels before heading into the living room and look out the window and wait for Joe. After a few minutes I see a car pull up and stop outside my gate and I smile as Joe walks out the car holding a bunch of white lilies so I run towards the door and open it when he presses the doorbell "hey" he holds the flowers out and I smile and take them "hi." I open the door and nod towards the living room "let me just get these in water and we can leave?" He nods and walks into the living room and I run into the kitchen grabbing a vase from under the sink and stick water into it and place it on the table sticking the flowers in. I walk into the living room and smile "ready?" Joe looks at me and nods "yeah" he looks around before following me out the door and towards his car. I get into his car and he starts the engine and drives down the street "I never knew you stayed in the old Magnum spies house" I smile and nod "yeah we moved there a few weeks ago" he looks at me and smirks "you like it?" I shrug and laugh nervously "it's nothing special but I like the town" he raises his eyebrow and smiles "so you haven't found the secret rooms?" I laugh nervously and shake my head looking towards the floor "I don't believe they are real" he smiles and shrugs "well if you find it then let me know" I nod firmly and smile "I will." After a few minutes he stops outside a building and smiles "hope you like Chinese?" I look towards it and nod "love it!" He gets out the car and I follow him inside where we are greeted by a man "table for 2?" He looks at Joe and he nods "yes please" the man walks towards a table and places menus down "can I get youse a drink while youse decide what to eat?" I sit down and smile "can I have a cola please?" He nods and looks at Joe "a beer" the man nods and walks away "a beer? Are you aloud to drink before work?" He shrugs and takes his jacket of "my dad owns the club I work in so he won't say anything." The man comes back carrying a tray with a can of cola and a beer on it "plus it's just one" he winks and holds his beer up "cheers?" I cheers his beer and smile "cheers" I pick the menu up and look through it. "So what made you and" I smile and look up "my cousin Roxy" he nods and leans back "what made you and your cousin Roxy move here?" I lean back and shrug "she picked the town I just tagged along" he smile and leans forward "do youse travel a lot?" I look at the menu and cough "we have been the last 2 years" he nods firmly and picks his menu up "work?" I smile and shake my head "no she just didn't settle anywhere but she said she likes it here so I guess we are staying" he smirks and nods "good!" The man comes back over and nods "ready to order?" I look at Joe and nod "yes." After dinner Joe stands up and holds his arm out "shall we?" I wrap my arm around his and walk outside and into his car. He drives down the street and stops after a few minutes outside a bar/club "Juicy J?" I get out the car and look towards it "didn't I mention? There is a stirp club inside" I shake my head and laugh nervously "no!" He rolls his eyes and holds his arm out "come on it's only one bit of the club" I wrap my arm around his and walk towards the door and towards a large man standing by the door "evening Joe" the man nods towards Joe and he smiles "evening Henry" the man opens the door and we walk in. I look around the large colourful hallway and see stairs at the end of the hallway "don't worry you won't see any the strippers" a door opens as we approach it and a woman wearing a skin-tight dress walks out and smiles "hey Joe!" She hugs him and he laughs nervously "hey T" she looks back into the door she came out of and laughs softly "hey girls Joe is here!" A group of girls run out all wearing skin-tight dresses and hugs Joe "sorry!" I shake my head and wave "I'm just going to grab a drink" he nods and smiles "ok!" The girls drag him into the room and close the door behind them "what way to the bar?" I look down the hallway and walk towards it and walk down the stairs and spot stripper poles and leather seats one side and fluffy pink seats the other side "wrong room" I laugh nervously and turn around. "You looking for the bar?!" I turn around and spot a woman wearing a bralette and shorts walking towards me "yeah" she laughs softly and points behind her "this way" I follow her towards the door at the back and she opens it and I see a large bar sigh "thank you" she smiles and nods "good luck" she looks me up and down before heading back out the door. I walk towards the bar and see a man standing smiling at me "hey" I sit down and smile "hi" he grabs a glass and nods "drink?" I look towards the fridge and smile "a beer please" he nods and laughs softly "ok." He grabs a beer and hands me it "so are you ready?" I look around and laugh nervously "for what?" The door opens and I see Joe "your interview?" I look at the man and laugh sarcastically "what?" Joe walks over laughing "dad! This is Amy" the man looks at Joe and shakes his head "of course your date" he looks at me and smiles "sorry I just thought" I look down and laugh nervously "it's fine." He walks out from the bar and hugs me "I'm John" he looks at Joe and smiles "his dad and the owner" I look around and smile "it's lovely." Joe walks behind the bar and grabs a bottle of beer "this is dads bar" he walks towards me and smiles "mine is upstairs" he wraps his arm around mine and I follow him out the door and towards the stairs. He walks through a door in the hallway and I see a large stripper pole in the middle of the large hall and seats all around with tables "this is where I work." I look towards the bar and smile "is this where the" he laughs softly and shakes his head "the girls work downstairs" he looks towards the pole and hands me his beer "this is just got entertainment" he runs towards it and does a spin "your turn" he walks towards me and takes the beers "what?" He nods towards the pole and I smile "really?" He nods and laughs softly "yeah" I sigh and nod "ok then" I run towards the pole and jump onto it swinging around it "wow!" I laugh nervously and walk towards him taking the beer "and that is how it's done." I walk towards the bar and he follows "you have skill" he walks behind the bar and smiles "if you ever need a job?" He looks around and nods firmly "come too me" I sit down and smile "thanks but I am good for now." I stick my beer down and he hands me a packet of nuts "make yourself at home" he looks towards the clock "it's about to get busy" he looks towards the door as it opens and I see a large man in a suite open the doors and make them stay open "open already?" I look at the clock and laugh "it's 8 already?!" I shake my head and down my beer "I should go!" He shakes his head and walks towards the fridge and grabs another beer before opening it "what?" I smile and look towards my phone "I told Roxy I would appear at this party" he hands me the beer and smiles "have another one before you go then?" I sigh and nod taking the beer "ok but just one" he nods towards a table at the side "go sit there and I will get one of the girls to come and keep you company?" He looks towards the door as a group of people walk in "don't leave without saying goodbye ok?" I nod and smile "ok" he raises his eyebrow and walks towards me "promise?" I smile and stand-up "I promise" he nods firmly and smile "good." I walk toward the table at the side and sit down as a group of people walk towards Joe and he serves them. I drink half the beer and my head instantly goes, my fingers and toes go numb and the room looks like it's spinning at 100mph. I look towards the bar and wave

"Joe I'm going to head home!" I see Joe look towards me and wave "wait 10 mins and I will get you out!" I nod and lean back "ok ok but only 10 minutes." A woman sits next to me and I feel her breath against my neck as they speak to me "are you ok?" I look at her and stick my thumb up "yeah I'm fine." She grabs my arm and around wraps it around her neck "let's get you home" I stand up and see someone approach us "I got her" I feel the girl let go of me slowly as if all into someone else arms and they carry me out the club and into a car. I look at them but can't make out their face and after a few seconds I blank out. I open my eyes again slightly and look at my arm and see my tied to a chair "what?" I open my eyes more and see a tattoo book on the table next to me "Juicy J tattoo studio" I shake my head and try free my hands "hello?!" I hear footsteps appear and I look at the door and it goes silent for a few seconds before the door comes flying of the hinges "Amy?!" I smile at the familiar voice "Brody?!" I look at the door and see Brody run in "how did you know I was here?" He runs towards me and rips the ties of from my hand and let's "I will explain everything after but for now follow me and stay close" he walks towards the door and I follow him and look outside and see men lying on the floor all up the hall unconscious "what happened?" Brody stops and pulls my close to him and against the wall "shh." He looks around the corner and looks at me "stay here" he goes around the corner and I shake my head "what? Don't leave me here" I look around the corner and see him sneaking up to a man by a door before pushing him softly but still sending him flying 'what?!' I go back behind the wall as Brody walks towards me "let's go!" I follow him towards the door with a lot of questions on my mind 'how did he find me? How did he make that big muscular man go unconscious with just a push? How did I get here?!' He opens the door and I see Jeremy's car outside "get in!" I run towards it and get in the back and see Liam "thank god you're ok!" He cuddles me and I smile "I'm fine" I look at Brody and sigh "I think." He closes the door and gets into the front "go!" Jeremy drives of and I look around as he drives out the estate and back towards my house. The journey back was silent and after we stopped Liam touched my hand and smiles "you ok?" I nod firmly and smile "yeah." He looks at Brody and nods "I will be inside" he gets out the car and I look at Brody "Jeremy give us a minute" Jeremy leaves the car and Brody turns around and smiles softly "so Joe Skinner? That's who you went out with?" I roll my eyes and open the car "goodbye Brody." He opens his door and shakes his head "I'm sorry" I turn around and sigh "you want to talk about the girl you was with?" He looks down and shakes his head "I don't even know her name so not really" I laugh sarcastically and shake my head "so you just slept with a random girl without knowing her name?" He smirks and shakes his head "I didn't sleep with her" I roll my eyes and walk towards my door "goodbye Broody!" I open the front door and close it behind me and run upstairs and into my room. I change into clean pj's and turn the light out before heading into bed and falling asleep straight away. The next morning I wake up and run downstairs and see Jennifer and Roxy sitting at the kitchen table "hey!" Jennifer looks at me and smiles "Amy!" She runs towards me and hugs me "are you ok?" I nod and smile "yes I'm fine but I have 101 questions." Roxy smiles softly and hugs me "I didn't want to wake up last night but it's good to have you back and I'm glad you're ok!" Jennifer nods towards the kitchen window behind me and smiles, I look over and see Brody standing there smiling "we will leave youse too it" Jennifer stands up and walks towards the kitchen door with Roxy and I take a deep breath and open the back door letting Brody in "can we start again?" I smile and nod "fine but I want to know what happened last night" I walk towards the kitchen door and smile "we can sit in my room" I look at my clothes and shrug "I need to get changed anyway." I walk up the stairs and he follows me into my room and sits on my bed as I grab clothes and head into the bathroom and get changed out of my pjs "so what happened?" I walk out and sit on the bed with him and he laughs nervously "Jennifer used to date Joe but they broke up for personal reasons and he didn't take it very well so he got someone to drug her and kidnapped her but luckily Liam stuck a tracker on her phone and we followed it to the tattoo studio you was in and we found Joe's brother Deano forcing alcohol down her throat so Liam beat him up pretty bad and we didn't hear anything from them again and when Roxy showed up without you earlier Jennifer asked where you was and she told her you had a date and Jennifer told us and we knew you was in trouble so Roxy managed to track your phone location and we found you in the same tattoo studio." I raise my eyebrows in shock and shake my head "Deano tried too" I look down and sigh "attack me at Ryder's party" Brody holds my hand and shakes his head "what do you mean attack you?" I smile softly and look into his eyes "he attacked Kim but I managed to get him of her and he turned on me" I could see his face turn angry and his muscles in his arm tensed up "he hit me a few times and I went unconscious and woke up in the bathroom and I see him speaking too someone and that's when I blew the whistle but he hit me again and stood on my leg before youse came" he let's go of my hands and stands up

"I'm going to kill him!" He walks towards the door and I stand up and run towards him "no wait!" I grab his arm and feel his muscles tense "he isn't worth doing jail time over." He turns around and takes a deep breath before grabbing me in for a cuddle "I am so sorry! I should have been there to comfort you instead of trying to make you jealous with another girl" I cuddle into him and sigh "it's ok. I'm ok" I hold onto him as tight as I can and smile and his arms squeeze me a little bit tighter. He let's go and holds me hand "come on" he walks down the stairs and I shake my head "where are we going?" He looks into the living room and waves "I'm borrowing Amy for a while but won't be out to late and I will take care of her." Roxy looks at me and smiles "I'm working after so I will see you after have fun" Brody walks out the door and I follow him towards his motorbike before getting on it and driving of down the street. He stops in the middle of the woods and smiles "come on" I get of the bike and he holds his hand out so I take it and follow him through the woods. He stops and smiles "ready?" I smirk and nod "for what?" He looks up the hill so I walk up and look over and see a large lake, blue as the sky and the sunlight hitting of it "wow!" I shake my head and walk towards him "it's beautiful" I look at Brody and smile "this is my favourite place to come when I'm angry" he looks towards the lake and smiles "come on." I follow him towards the lake and he picks up a stone and flings it towards the water and it hits of it a few times "it's nice and peaceful" he looks at me and as I look into his amazing green eyes I can't help but blush, I wanted him and I couldn't keep it to myself anymore. I take a deep breath and walk towards him "I love it" I hold onto his arms and lean into his face and kiss him. Luckily he kisses me back and he wraps his arms around my waist and my whole body falls at his touch 'this was the best feeling ever and I never wanted it to end.' As I pull away I feel his hands hold onto my tightly and he pulls me back into kiss him more "we should go" I laugh softly and shake my head "after I show you something" he holds my hand and walks along the lake and towards the pier. He stops at the end of the pier and smirks before sitting down "sit with me?" I sit down and he wraps his arm around me and pulls me in for a cuddle "I'm sorry" I look at him and shake my head "for what?" He looks towards the lake and shrugs "everything? Not telling you how I felt and hurting you with that girl" I look into the water and smirk "what makes you think you hurt me with her?" He looks at me and smiles "Roxy told me" I look at him and roll my eyes "of course she did." He stands up and offers me his hands "thanks" he pulls he up and kisses my forehead before wrapping his arm around mine "let's get food." I smile and nod firmly "I like you're thinking" I follow him back towards the motorbike and he hands me the helmet and I get on the back and hold tightly onto him as he drives of. We get to the bottom of the lake entrance and I spot a black truck with black out windows packed at the bottom but it starts as soon as we pass it and follows us for about half a mile before I tap Brody's shoulders and he pulls over at the side of the road and the car drives towards us before slowing down and gets closer towards us. The car eventually reaches us and I look at it as it drives closer the closer to us it gets before eventually hitting the bike hard sending me and Brody flying over the side railing and down a hill.

I feel the helmet smash of a rock as I hit the bottom of the hill "Brody?!" I quickly get up and run towards Brody and see him unconscious on the floor with his head bleeding "Brody!" I take my helmet of and look back up the hill and see an older looking man lift Brody's motorbike up like it was a toy and fling it down the hill before getting back into the car and driving off. I look as the bike comes flying down the hill towards us "shit!" I grab Brody's arm's and pull them as hard as I can dragging his whole body out the way of the bike but as I see it a few inches away I kneel down towards Brody's body and put the helmet back on before covering him and eventually the bike hits me sending me flying across the woods and I land on my belly with the bike on top of me before going unconscious.

When I finally come back around I open my eyes and see I'm in the hospital so I panic and quickly get out of the bed and head towards the door. I see Brody outside walking towards me with looking towards the ground so I quickly look down the hallway and run towards the exit. I look around the hospital hallway for the main entrance and sigh 'please don't let him see me!' I spot the main entrance at the bottom of the stairs so I run down them and head out the door and towards the taxi's. I get into the taxi as Brody walks out the entrance and I look the other way "drive!" The taxi drives of and I take a deep breath as I look back towards the hospital and see Brody on his phone looking around. The taxi pulls up outside my house and I look at the drive and smile "give me a minute" he nods firmly and I run into the house and see Roxy in the living room with Jeremy who is on the phone. They both look at me and Roxy takes a deep breath and smiles "thank god!" Jeremy nods and smiles "she just walked through the door" Roxy hugs me and I smile "you need to pay the taxi" she looks outside and nods "ok" she runs out and I smile and look at Jeremy as he comes of the phone "where did you go?" I smile and walk towards the sofa sitting down "I panicked." Bear comes running in and jumps up on the sofa licking my face and hands "hey boy!" I stick him on my knee and stroke his head "why did you panic?" Roxy walks in and shakes her head "in case Brody realised the name" Roxy rolls her eyes and scoffs "I gave the hospital your details because he didn't know them all so you have nothing to worry about" I take a deep breath and look towards the window as I hear a motorbike pull up "what will I tell him?" Jeremy smiles and walks towards the door "leave it to me" he looks at the door and shrugs "I will tell him your sleeping or something so don't want any visitors" I smile and nod "ok thank you." I look back towards the window and sigh "can you tell him I'm sorry? For everything" Jeremy shakes his head and laughs softly "you saved his life Amy." I walk towards the sofa and sit down as Jeremy leaves "you ok?" I look at Roxy as she walks towards me and sits down "just a few bruises but I'm ok" she smiles softly and rubs my arm "you was out for 2 days" I raise my eyebrow and shake my head "what?" I laugh nervously and she nods "we was on the way to the hospital with clean clothes because the doctor knew you would come around today but Brody called Jeremy and said you had disappeared so he thought that whoever hit youse with the car came to the hospital and for a second I thought it was Nathan" I hold her hand and shake my head "I'm sorry" she squeezes my hand and smiles "you're ok now though that's all that matters." She stands up and walks toward the door and I follow her "so who was the people in the car?" She walks into the kitchen and shrugs "Jeremy thinks it was Joe so he went to pay him a visit and he said it wasn't him and he learned his lesson so we don't know." I take a deep breath and grab a bottle of water "well I'm going for a wash and a sleep" I head towards the kitchen door and Roxy smiles and nods firmly "ok sweetie." I run upstairs and into my bedroom and grab clean pjs before heading for a shower. As the water runs down my back I can just see blood in my mind, I see the bike flying towards me and Brody's moveless body and I jump and turn the shower of. I head into the bedroom and get changed before towel drying my hair and open window letting some air in and get into bed before drifting off to sleep. I wake up a few hours later with the sun shining into my bedroom window, I look towards my alarm clock and yawn "only 4PM?" I get out of bed and get changed before heading downstairs. I walk into the kitchen and smile "Roxy?" I see a pizza box on the table so I eat a slice and walk towards the window and grab a glass and see Liam outside cleaning the shed. I walk towards the back door and unlock it and walk towards the fence "what ya doing?" He jumps dropping a shovel "god you scared me!" He sticks the shovels back inside the shed and closes it "was helping Brody cleaned but he left halfway through because he got a phone call" I look towards the house and shrug "so where is he now?" He looks towards the front yard and smirks. I follow his eyes and see a bike pull up and see Brody taking his helmet of "here we go" Liam looks towards me and smiles "good luck" he walks towards the house and walks inside as Brody walks towards me shaking his head. "I know! I'm sorry" he climbs the fence and grabs me into him and holds onto my body tightly "I'm so glad you're ok!" I smile and sink into his arms and take a deep breath "so you're not mad?" He looks at me and shakes his head "I was but no. I'm just glad you're ok and safe" I smile softly and hug him for a few more seconds. He takes my hand and leads me inside the house and into the living room "let's watch a movie while Roxy and Jeremy are out" he sits down and I sit down next to him and cuddle into him as he turns the TV on. He starts a movie and after a few seconds the front door opens and Bear runs in "and that will be the end of that" Roxy and Jeremy walk in and smile "what are you kids doing?" I look at Roxy and smile "just watching a movie." She looks at Brody and smirks "hmm!" She holds a bag up and smiles "well we are going out tonight so go get changed" she flings me the bag and I pull out a black dress "where?" She smirks and shrugs "just for food" I raise my eyebrows and scoff "the last time we done this you told me about" I smirk and look at Jeremy "won't be long!" I run upstairs and into my room before quickly getting changed. I run back downstairs and grab my heels and my bag and look towards Roxy and shrug "let's go!" She rolls her eyes and kisses Jeremy "bye" she follows me out the house and into her car. I look at her with eager eyes and take a deep breath "so are you?" She looks at me and smiles "what?" I roll my eyes and look at her hand "pregnant?!" She smiles and nods "yes but you can't tell Brody" I grin ear to ear and nod "ok but why?" Roxy coughs and shakes her head "it's complicated but I'm sure Brody will tell you in his own time" I raise my eyebrows and shake my head "I don't even care why. I'm just so excited!" She pulls into a car park and smiles "ready?" I look around and laugh nervously "to go where?" She smirks and gets out the car "follow me." I get out the car and follow her towards an old look church "this is where Jeremy took me for our first date" I smirk and head in as she opens the door "it looks lovely." I walk in and see a large open space with chairs and tablets everywhere and 2 bars at each side "table for 2?" I look towards the side and see a woman standing "yeah" she leads towards a table and sits down two menus "have youse been here before?" Roxy nods and smiles "yeah I have" she nods and sticks a button down "ok well just buzz me when you're ready" she smiles at me before walking away. "Buzz her?" I look at the button and Roxy nods and sits down "yes it's a way for them to know you're ready to order" I shake my head and laugh softly "weird but ok" I sit down and smile at her "so when you getting the ring?" She smirks and goes into her bag pulling out a ring box "I got it already but Jeremy wants me to hold back wearing it until he tells Brody" she opens the box and I smile at it "wow! It's beautiful" she closes It and sticks it back in her bag "Jeremy is going to tell Brody this weekend at his birthday weekend away" I smile and lean back "what you got Jeremy for his birthday?" Roxy laughs sarcastically and shakes her head "what?" I smile nervously and shake raises her eyebrows "it's Brody's birthday?" I laugh nervously and shake my head "is it?" She smirks and leans forward "Jeremy has planned a birthday weekend for him at his parents log cabin? He didn't tell you?" I shrug and lean forward "he hasn't told me anything." I pick up the menu and take a deep breath "can we get drinks?" Roxy picks her menu up and smiles "what you wanting?" I look at her and shrug "cocktail?" She rolls her eyes and presses the button "fine but just this once" I smile and lean back sticking the menu back down as the woman comes back "what can I get youse?" Roxy smiles and holds the drink menu up "two of your best cocktails please" the woman doesn't even look at me before nodding at Roxy and walks away "so about this weekend away." The rest of the evening goes by with a flow as we have some girly time and talk about everything including Brody's birthday and the wedding. After a few, ok a lot of cocktails the waitress comes back over and smiles "can I get youse some food or will youse be just having more cocktails?" I smile and look at her "can we get a large bowl of chicken wings and chips?" She nods and smiles "oh and two more cocktails" she nods and walks away and I look at Roxy as her phone goes "it's Jeremy" she stands up and smiles "I will be two minutes" She stands up and walks towards the exit and I lean back onto my chair. The waitress comes back over and smiles "these are from the gentlemen over there" she points towards the bar and I see Joe and Deano "tell him I don't want them" I hand her them back and she smiles "of course" she heads back over and I watch her as she gives the cocktails to them. Joe looks over and smiles evilly like he was trying to get to me but I shook my head and looked towards the exit where Roxy disappeared to. After a few minutes I see Roxy come in smiling "what you smiling at?" She sits down and shrugs "I told Jeremy that you never even knew it was Brody's birthday but he said that Brody was going to tell you tonight before we walked in and was going to invite you himself" I smile softly and lean back "really?" She nods firmly and smiles "guess he does like you" I roll my eyes and stand up "I'm going to the bathroom so don't eat all the chicken wings before I get back ok?" She nods and smiles "I can't promise anything" I laugh nervously and look back towards Joe and Deano sitting at the bar before looking back at Roxy and shake my head "oh and Joe and Deano are here but don't cause a scene ok? Bye" I quickly walk towards the bathroom leaving her looking around. I come out the bathroom cubical and wash my hands and look in the mirror but jump when I see Joe standing behind me smiling "what are you doing here?!" He smirks and walks towards me "I missed you" I walk towards the door but he stops me and shakes his head "now what's the rush?" He goes into his pocket and pulls out his phone "wouldn't want anything bad happening to Roxy now would we?" He shows me the screen and I see Deano standing outside with a woman with black curly hair like Roxy's lying on the ground unconscious "what have you done to her?" I grab his phone but he moves to fast "now now that's not going to happen!" He smirks and I shake my head and lean back onto the sink "what do you want?" He hands me a brown envelope and smiles "I want you to make Brody a cake for his birthday this weekend and you can give him it at his parents log cabin" he winks and I shake my head and open the package "how did you know about that?" He stops me opening it and smiles "I heard you" I laugh sarcastically and shake my head "how? You was sitting at the bar so no way you could have heard us." He rolls his eyes and walks towards the door "so you still don't know? I have the same abilities as your boyfriend" I scoff and shake my head "what abilities? He is nothing like you" he smirks and opens the bathroom door "just mix that in with his cake" I look at the envelope and smile "no" he rolls his eyes and walks towards me "don't make this more difficult" I step back and look at the envelope and smirk before opening it and pulling out a green mixture before smashing it onto the ground "you are going to wish you never done that" Joe smirks before heading towards the door "goodbye!" He leaves and I look at the green mixture spilled on the floor and bend down as it starts to glow "what did he give me?" Smoke starts coming out from it and I quickly stand up and run towards the bathroom door and pull it but it doesn't move "Joe!" I look back towards the mixture as a small fire appears "shit!" I look towards the window at the other side of the bathroom and run towards it and climb onto the sink but the bars are sealed tight "help!" I bang on the window and look back towards the door and see the fire growing bigger and faster. The fire alarm goes off and the sprinklers kick in but the fire doesn't even budge and makes it worse. I run into a bathroom cubical and look at my phone when it rings and see Roxy's name appear "Roxy?" I wait a few seconds and hear her voice "hey there's been a fire so I'm outside so come out now" I look at the fire and take a deep breath "I know I'm trapped in the bathroom where the fire is" I close the cubical door again and close my eyes "don't worry you are going to be ok" she hangs up and I shake my head "don't come back in here!" I look around the bathroom and spot a black jumper by the sink so I quickly grab it and hold it around my mouth but after a few seconds I go unconscious and fall to the hot floor hitting my head. As I lay on the floor unconscious Roxy rings Jeremy "there has been a fire and Amy is trapped inside!" Not knowing Brody is listening he runs out the house and jumps on his motorbike and quickly drives the fastest he cans towards the restaurant. I open my eyes when I feel someone lift me up and open my eyes and see Brody "Brody?" He smiles towards me and nods "shh it's ok" I look around and see nothing insight, I look down and see lights above us and Brody floating in the air before going unconscious again in his arms.

I feel myself come back around and I quickly open my eyes and sit up "Brody?" I see Brody sitting at the bottom of my bed "hey!" He runs towards my side and smiles "how you feeling?" I look around and shake my head "how did I get here?" He smiles and sits beside me "I brought you home" I smile and hug him "I remember" he looks at me and laughs nervously "what do you remember exactly?" I look at him and shake my head "nothing really" he smiles softly and nods "well you get some rest and I will check on you tomorrow?" I nod and he kisses me and stands up and walks towards the door "bye" I smile softly and wave "bye" he leaves and I wait a few seconds before grabbing the black folder and open it. I start reading more of the files and lean back placing the folder down "he can't be! Can he?" I look towards the window and sigh "can Brody James really be the person the person the Magnum spies where talking about in this file?" I shake my head and stand-up "I need air." I grab the set of keys from my drawer and my camera and run downstairs grabbing my backpack before heading out the door and towards the woods. 'He can't be? He seems so normal' I look towards the sky and take a deep breath 'but on the other hand I know what I saw last night and he did get to me really fast' I turn into the woods and stop "Joe said he had the same abilities as him? I wonder if he was talking about that?" I walk into the woods and towards the cottage the spies bodies are 'I need more answers!' I reach the entrance for the house and when I get inside I start looking for more files or anything that can help me with my answers and I spot the cupboard with with lock and grab the keys from my pocket and walk towards it and try the keys. Eventually one fits and it unlocks "please let there be something down here" I take a deep breath before opening the door and heading inside.

I turn the torch on my phone on and spot a switch on the side of the wall so I turn it on and see a large steel room with a large TV and 4 small TV's beside it and a sofa opposite the TV's. I spot 3 large steel drawers so I walk towards the drawers and open it and see loads of folders with different file numbers on them so I grab a file and walk towards the sofa and open it "File 5." I turn the page and see a recipe "weakness position" I look at the drawing on the page and spot a blue flower and red thorns so I look around the room and spot 8 plant pots under a mini greenhouse in the corner with blue flowers and red thorns. "The red thorn flower is known to weaken the UC (Unknown creatures) and could possibly kill them if near it long enough" I take a deep breath and fling my head back "this doesn't prove Brody is one!" I flip through the book and stop at a page and smile "UC suspects" I go down the list of names and stop "Jeremy and Brody James" I shake my head and laugh nervously "I knew it!" I look back at the list and scoff "John, Joe, Dean and Abbie Skinner" I shake my head and grab my phone from my pocket and ring Brody who answers after the 2nd ring "missing me already?" I laugh softly and look back towards the book "quick question" I lean back and take a deep breath "what is your ex-girlfriends Abbie's second name?" After a long pause I hear him laugh nervously "Skinner why?" I look back towards the book and place my finger on Abbie's name "just curious" I hang up before he can say another word and turn my phone on silent before placing it back into my pocket. I look at the list of names and take a deep breath "so the town is filled with people with powers including my own boyfriend? Great!" I close the book and stick it back into the drawer and grab another "surely one of these will tell me more about the flowers?" I flick through another file number 2 and smile "bingo!" I read through the page and nod "so the flowers can live without sunlight and water when fully grown? That's good to know." I close the book and walk towards the flowers "so these will weaken him?" I shake my head and step back "he would never hurt me, would he?" I look at the plants and shrug "maybe not but Joe or Deano would!" I pull the cover of them and grab all 8 of them and grab 2 other files and stick them in my bag with the flowers before heading back upstairs and out the front door and back towards my house. I get outside and see Brody on his bike just driving of down the street the opposite way so I sigh and run towards the house and run upstairs. I get into my room and place my backpack onto the bed and take the flowers out and place them under my bed in a box and place the folders and the folder on my bed in my drawer before heading back downstairs. "Morning" I look into the living room and see Roxy "hey" she taps the sofa next to her and smirks "want to talk about last night?" I smile and nod firmly "I'm fine I don't remember much all I know is Brody was here when I woke up and he said he brought me back." She raises her eyebrow and shakes her head "so you don't know how the fire started or how you got locked in the bathroom?" I shake my head and laugh nervously "no I don't know I passed out after you I hanged up the phone with you" she smiles softly and hugs me "I'm just glad you're ok." I stand up and walk towards the kitchen "I'm going to make dinner about 6 and Jeremy and Brody are coming over so can you help set the table?" I smile softly and nod "ok" I run upstairs and look at one of the flowers "guess we will soon know if he is one when I place this in the middle of the table" I smirk and grab a plant pot and run downstairs and place it onto the kitchen table. Roxy walks in and smiles "Jeremy is just getting wine and they will be over so let's get the table set" she grabs a tray of lasagne from the oven and places it in the middle of the table "nice flowers" I smirk and grab plates "I got them from the woods." I set the plates down and the doorbell goes "they are here" she runs towards the door and opens it "just through the kitchen" I cough and stand up straight smiling as they walk in "hey" Brody hugs me and kisses my forehead "you ok?" I smile and nod firmly "yeah you?" He looks around and nods "yeah." He looks at Jeremy and smirks "did you bring that thing?" Jeremy laughs nervously and shakes his head "what thing?" He rolls his eyes and walks towards him and whispers in his ear. Jeremy nods firmly and looks at Roxy "can you excuse us?" Roxy nods and they both walk out the front door and I look at Roxy and shrug "what was that about?" Roxy laughs nervously and shrugs "not sure." She places the lasagne onto plates and grabs 2 colas and 2 beers from the fridge and places them on the table "I'm sure they will be back in a second." I walk into the living room and look out the window and see Brody and Jeremy in the garden talking before Jeremy hands Brody something and they eat it and smile before heading back towards the door. I run into the hallway and smile when the doorbell goes "I will get it" I open the door and smirk "get it?" Jeremy laughs nervously and holds up his phone "yeah" I look at his phone and smile "well welcome back" they walk in and I follow them into the kitchen. "This smells amazing" Jeremy sits at the table and I watch him reach across the table and grab his beer while touching the flower without flinching. I smirk and sit down "so let's eat!" I sit next to Brody and he hands me a can of cola and also touches the flower and I smirk "thank you" he nods firmly and smiles "your welcome." As we eat dinner I watch Jeremy and Brody closely and see if they react to the flower but they don't 'it's either not working or they are not one of them.' Jeremy looks at the flower and smiles "that's pretty" Roxy looks at me and nods "Amy found it in the woods" they both look at me and I smile nervously "really?" I nod and look at it "yeah it was just lying there and I thought it would be nice in the kitchen to lighten the place up a bit." Jeremy smiles and nods "it's lovely" I smirk and nod "thank you."

After dinner Jeremy helps Roxy take the plates away and Brody stands up and holds his hand out and nods towards the back door so I take his hand and follow him out and he sits on the grass "you ok?" I smile and sit next to him "yeah just tired" he smirks and nods. The rest of the afternoon we sit out the back and talk and before I know it I spot the sun setting "I should probably go." Brody stands up and I smile and stand up nodding "ok" he moves towards me and kisses my forehead "I will see you tomorrow?" I smirk and nod "ok" he walks towards the fence and climbs it "we can take the dogs to the beach or something? Take a lunch basket" I smile and nod "that sounds perfect" he walks inside and I take a deep breath and smile "at least I can cross him of the list." I head back inside and see Jeremy and Roxy kissing on the sofa "gross!" I shake my head and run upstairs and run the shower "Amy?!" I look in my bedroom and see Roxy "yeah?" She looks at me and smiles "me and Jeremy are going to the cabin tonight to clean it for tomorrow so you going to be ok here yourself tonight?" I smile and nod "yeah I'm just going to have a shower and call it a night anyway" she smirks and waves "ok I will see you tomorrow" she walks out the door closing it slightly behind her and I turn my radio on before heading into the shower. I hear a loud bang from my bedroom that makes me jump "Roxy?!" I turn the shower of and grab my dressing gown and go check it out. I see my bedside drawer open and paper lying all around the floor "Roxy?!" I look out the hallway but no one replies so I grab my phone and ring Roxy but goes straight to voicemail. I look towards my window and see it wide open with the curtains blowing in "hello?" I look around and grab my dancing trophy as a weapon and walk towards my window but no one is there so I close and lock it and look under the bed "hello?" I take a deep breath and stick the trophy down and grab pjs before sticking them on and fix the pieces of paper lying on the floor and stick them back into the drawer and lock it and tape the key under the drawer.

I head downstairs and lock the back door and grab a can of cola before locking the front door and heading back upstairs and stick a DVD on before getting into bed. I watch the fire hour of the movie before drifting off to sleep for a few minutes but wake back up when I hear a loud bang "Roxy?!" I jump out of bed and run into the hallway "Roxy?!" I shake my head and take a deep breath before heading back towards my bedroom. I close the door slightly behind me and get into bed "hello Amy!" I jump and look towards the bathroom and see Joe and Deano standing at the bathroom door "what are youse doing here?" The look at each and smirk "just finish what we started" I look at the window and back at them before running towards the window and quickly open it "Brody!" The run towards me and Joe grabs me back while Deano closes the window "you shouldn't have done that!" Joe flings me onto the floor and I look under my bed and spot the flowers "what do youse want with me?" Still looking at the flowers I see them walk towards me so I quickly grab one of the flowers and hold it in front of me "where did you get that?!" The back away and hold their nose "I don't my research" I smirk and walk towards them "this isn't over!" Joe opens the window and they both disappear out it "I have plenty more flowers don't worry!" I close and lock the window and see Brody's room light on and spot him running outside and towards my house "Brody?!" He looks up and shakes his head "you ok?" I smile and nod "bad dream" he looks around and nods "you sure?" I laugh nervously and nod "yeah I'm going back sleep so I will speak to you tomorrow" he nods and looks towards his bedroom "I will keep my window open ok?" I smile and wave "ok, night" I head towards the TV and turn it off before heading back into bed and turn my lamp of. As I drift back of too sleep I glance at the door one more time and see a shadow behind the door making me jump up "who's there?!" The door swings open and I see Joe standing holding a green mixture "this time you won't get away" he smirks and quickly gets beside my side and pulls my arm "let's see what lover boy will do now." He grabs my arm and pulls me towards the window and opens it "Brody!" I see Brody quickly appear and turn his light on before opening his window full "let her go!" He has an evil look in his eyes and they turn red "ready for the show?" Joe looks at me and I shake my head "let me go!" He laughs sarcastically and shakes his head "not going to happen sorry" he moves closer to me and forces his lips onto mine before picking me up "catch!" He looks at Brody and smirks before hanging me over the window ledge and dangling my feet down "STOP!" I hold onto his hand for dear life and as I feel him fight my hand away I look at Brody as he lets go of me and I start to fall to the ground. I close my eyes tight as I float through the air and get ready to hit the hard concreate at the bottom but instead I feel strong warm hands wrap around my waist 'was this all in my head? Was it a dream? Did Joe really fling me out the window?' Too scared to open my eyes I lean into the warm body and hold onto them tightly "I'm sorry." I open my eyes when I hear Brody's voice "I knew it!" I look around and see us flying across the sky "why didn't you say anything if you knew?" I laugh nervously and shrug "I don't know" he smiles and shakes his head "where are you taking me?" He looks in front and takes a deep breath "somewhere safe" I lean into him as he fly's through the air like it was a normal thing. After a few minutes he looks down and takes a deep breath "hold on, we have company" he looks behind him and I follow his eyes and spot Joe and Deano flying behind us "we need to lose them." I look down and nod "loose them in the woods and I know the perfect place to go" he looks behind him and nods "I will see is Jeremy is busy" he turns his ring and the red crystal lights up "it's me" he looks behind him and takes a deep breath "code red" he looks at me and smiles softly "ok bye." He turns the ring again and nods "Jeremy is on his way so he will help distract them" he laughs softly and holds onto my tightly "hold on" I told onto his arms as he drives down "are they following us?" I look up and see them coming down behind us "yeah" I see them look straight and I follow their eyes and see Jeremy coming towards them really fast before grabbing onto them both and dragging them across the sky with him "we lost them." Brody stops and looks up "let's get you to the safe house" I shake my head and nod towards the way we came from "the house I was in was built for a safe house so go back there" he laughs nervously and shakes his head "the stories about the spies are just a tale" I shake my head and smile nervously "no it's real. They knew about you and that's how I found out" he raises his eyebrow and smirks "show me!" He flies back towards the house and into my window "how did you even find it?" He places me down and I walk towards my drawer where the key is and open the drawer and grab the files "it was by accident actually" I show him the files and laugh nervously "both times." He looks at the folders and shakes his head "I can't believe how much they knew and that no one actually believed them" he looks at me and smiles "so where did you find these?" I smirk and nod towards the door "I will show you." I take his hand and lead him towards the back yard and nod "stay here" I walk towards the secret entrance and open it "wow!" Brody comes running over "how long have you known about this?" I head down the ladders and smile "a while." He follows me down and looks around "I can't believe this has been here the whole time" he walks towards the TV screens and nods "is this live?" I smile and nod "yeah" I walk towards the drawer and open it "this is where I got the file and there is more in the cabin" he looks at me with curious eyes and smirks "cabin?" I smile and nod "yeah they have a hidden cabin in the woods" I look down and laugh nervously "they are actually still in it." Brody raises his eyebrows and shakes his head "what? You went in there while they was in it?" I look at him and shake my head "they aren't alive" he laughs sarcastically and I shrug "want to see?" He looks around before heading towards the ladder "yeah" I shake my head and push the ladder up "let's go out the other way" he looks around and scoffs "what other way?" I nod towards the secret door and smile "follow me." I walk towards it and lead him out through the tunnel and into the living room "you need to promise me if Joe and Deano come back that you will hide in here?" I smile and push the fireplace back into place "I will." I smile at him and nod "stay here" I run upstairs and grab the set of keys and run back downstairs smiling "ready?" He walk towards the front door and nods "let's take the bike because I don't know the way flying" he laughs nervously and nods "good idea" he walks towards his motorbike and I follow and sit on the back of it and he drives of towards the woods. I direct him through the woods and when I spot the sheets I point towards them and he drives over and stops "this way." I lead him inside but he stops at the door and falls to the ground "Brody!" I run up the stairs and lean down beside him "what's wrong?" He looks around and points towards the stairs "there's red thorn" I look over and spot a rug "this?" I pick it up and he nods so I run out the door with it and fling it in the woods "you ok?" He takes a deep breath and stands up "yeah but that was strong" I smile and hold his hand "I got you" he smirks and squeezes my hand "good." I head downstairs and into the kitchen and Brody let's go of my hand and looks around "the walls are all made with titanium so I can't see through them" I smirk and shake my head "you can see through walls?" He nods and smiles "yeah" I raise my eyebrow and smirk "all walls?" He winks and walks towards the living room "Brody!" I laugh nervously and follow him "is this them?" He walks towards the fireplace and grab the photos "you never met them?" He shakes his head and smiles "no they kept themselves too themselves and left by time I was old enough" I shake my head and smirk "well they must have known you because you are on the list?" He sticks the photos down and laughs sarcastically "list?" I nod and walk back into the kitchen and towards the basement door "down here." I open the door and look at Brody who falls onto the floor and passes out "Brody?!" I run towards him and catch his head before it hits the ground. I look towards the door for more red thorn's and I spot a spray on the top of the door with green mixture spraying out "please tell me that just sends you too sleep?" I look at Brody and take a deep breath before standing up and running into the basement and grabbing as many files as I can and running back upstairs closing the door behind me. I stick the files on the coffee table in the living room and run back into the kitchen and lift Brody's arms up and drag him into the living room, I take the sheets of the sofa before lifting him onto it.

Twenty minutes pass and Brody still doesn't wake up or move so I grab another folder and read through it "green mixture. Green mixture" I stop at a page with the heading 'Viridi Planetae soil' I begin to read it as Brody lays unconscious next to me. "Viridi Planetae translating into Green Planet is a planet where soil grown, the soil that the Unknown Creatures are afraid of. The soil will kill any UC if inhaled enough or can send them unconscious for a few hours. The dust was cleaned up when they knew that certain other creatures knew about it and used it against them leaving only a few bottles left." I look towards the kitchen and walk into it and take the spray of the wall but stop when I hear a click "Brody?" I look towards the living room and hear another click coming from under me. I look down and see the ground open up and see something come out of it and before I could bend down and check what it was I feel hands touch my arm and pull me into the living room. I hear a gun shot and look behind me and see Brody "how did you know that was going to happen?" He smirks and shrugs "they didn't stick titanium in the floorboards so I spotted the boggy trap when we came in. I hug him and smile "thank you" he holds onto my tightly and I take a deep breath "are you ok?" He looks towards the spray and nods "yeah but please get rid of that" he covers his mouth and I nod "I will." I head towards the stairs and nod "coming?" Brody nods and follows me upstairs "stay here" I head into the bathroom filled with spiderwebs and close the door behind me "please work." I open the spray and take the bottle of mist out and stick it down the sink and run some water, I watch it go down and smile "yes!" Once the dust disappears I look around and spot a bin so I open it and spot a piece of paper so I take it out and stick it in my pocket and place the bottle and spray in the bin and close it before heading back into the hallway with Brody and closing the bathroom door. Brody opens the bedroom door opposite the bathroom and I shake my head "you really don't want to go in there" he looks at me and laughs nervously "why?" He looks inside and spots Sharon on the bed "eww" he quickly closes the door and looks towards the hallway "I'm guessing the other one is down there?" I smile softly and nod "yip." He takes a deep breath and nods towards the stairs "this place would be a good safe house" he looks towards the bedroom door and shrugs "if the place didn't have dead people in it." He looks at me and smirks "what?" He shrugs and looks towards the bathroom "you want to start cleaning downstairs? I will get rid of the bodies and come help?" I laugh nervously and shake my head "your being serious?" He shrugs and looks towards the bedroom door "why not?" I take a deep breath and shrug "sure, why not." I head towards the stairs but Brody pulls me back and kisses me "what was that for?" I blushes and shrugs his shoulders "just because" I kiss him back and smile "what are you going to" I shake my head and laugh nervously "I don't even want to know what you are going to do." I head downstairs and look around "let's start with the kitchen" I head into the kitchen and find a radio so I walk towards it and turn it on "please work" I press the play button and the radio starts "yes!" I smirk and look around the kitchen "where do I even begin?" I take a deep breath and spot bin bags so I start binning the rubbish and old papers laying around before heading towards the cupboard beside the door and grab the brush and start brushing. I grab cleaning products from under the sink and grab a sponge and soak it in water and soap and start cleaning the kitchen worktops and table. I look around and take a deep breath "not too bad!" I grab the cleaning products and walk into the living room as Brody walks downstairs smiling "done" I laugh nervously and shake my head "I don't even want to know what you done with them." I head towards the fireplace and stick the cleaning products down and grab the white sheet of the sofas. "Kitchen is done so let's start in here" he looks around and nods "I will find a brush." I nod towards the kitchen and smile "it's in there" he nods firmly and heads into the kitchen and grabs the brush. I smile and shake my head before shaking down the pillows on the sofa and dust the place down.

After what seems like forever we finally finish and the whole house and I look at the bed where the dead body was and shake my head "we should bin that bedding and" I turn around and smirk when I see Brody standing with new bedding "one step ahead" he hands me one and nods towards the bed "I will do the other bed" I smile softly and nod "ok." He walks down the hallway and I turn around and walk towards the bed "eww!" I take a deep breath before taking the bedding of the bed and change it "can't believe the smell is still there." Brody walks in laughing softly "I will bind them" I smile and hand him the sheet "thank you" he takes the sheet and heads downstairs "you want to do the bathroom and let me know once it's done in case the place is still infected?" I smile and nod "ok" he runs downstairs and I wait a few seconds before heading into the bathroom "thank god this is the last room" I close the door behind me and look around "If I need to clean anytime soon again I will turn into a sponge!" I begin to clean the bathroom down and find an air freshener "bingo!" I grab it and spray it before heading out into the hallway closing the door behind me. "Brody?!" I look down the stairs and shake my head "I wonder where he is sticking them" I shake my head and walk towards the bedrooms spraying the air freshener before heading downstairs and spraying the rest of the house. I head downstairs and stick the brush and cleaning products back before heading back upstairs and picking the bin bags up and heading downstairs with them. "There's a bin outside" I jump and drop the bags "god! Brody!" I turn around and shake my head "you scared me" he laughs softly and walks towards me "sorry." He pushes a strand of hair behind my ear and kisses me cheek "let's get these bins out then head back and check in on Jeremy and Roxy" I smile and nod "ok." I grab the bag and he walks into the kitchen and grabs the bags from there before heading toward the front door and opening it "come on" I follow him out and he walks towards a big bin and places the bags in. I walk back Inside and look around "place looks not that bad now" he smirks and shrugs "could even be nice enough to live in" I choke and laugh nervously "you? What is living next to me that bad?" He laughs sarcastically and shrugs "I meant us" I laugh nervously and look down "what would living WITH me be that bad?" I shake my head and smile at him "no" He smirks and shakes his head "let's go." We get back to my house and I spot Liam outside with Bella so Brody flies down towards him "hey!" He jumps and turns around as Brody reaches the ground "what you doing?" He raises his eyebrows at Brody and I laugh nervously "I will leave youse too it" I turn around and head into my back door leaving them in the garden. I walk towards the fridge and grab a bottle of water before heading towards the kitchen window and look towards them. I take a sip of my water but nearly spit it out when I hear something behind me "Roxy?!" I quickly turn around and see Joe and Deano "hello again" Deano gives me an evil smirk and they walk towards me "stay back!" I look towards the back window and shake my head "Brody is right outside so stay there or I will scream and he will come in." The look at each other before shaking their heads "but he is a little tired to hear you?" I look out the window and see a woman smiling at me as she stands over Liam and Brody's bodies as they lay on the grass unconscious. "What have you done?" I look back towards Joe and Deano and Joe holds up a small portion of green mixture "don't worry" he looks at me and smirks "we have been giving orders not to kill them" he shrugs and sticks the mixture back into his pocket "yet." He nods towards Deano and he smirks and walks towards me "let's go!" He grabs my arm and pulls me out the kitchen, as I try fight him he grabs onto my arm tighter "your hurting me" he rolls his eyes and lets me go "move then!" I walk in front of him and follow Joe towards the front door. He opens the door and I look outside and spot a blacked out window jeep "where are you taking me?" Joe pushes me out and shakes his head "just go" I walk towards the car and it opens as I get too it and see a familiar face "you!" Joe pushes me into the car and shakes his head "move! We don't have all day" he gets into the car and closes it behind him and the car drives of down the road. I look to the familiar face and shake my head "why are you doing this?" The stick their hood down and he fix's his blonde slick hair "it's not personal." I shake my head and look around me "what do you mean it's not personal? Brody is your best friend Noah!" He looks at me and smiles "it was all an act to get close to him" I shake my head and disbelief and scoff "why?" He rolls his eyes and leans on the window "someone shut her up!" I feel something silk go around my mouth and a few seconds later I pass out.

I wake up in a dark cave with just a chair and a torch fire "hello?" I stand up and move but get pulled back with the chains on my wrist. "Hello?!" I try pull the chains a few times but they don't budge "I wouldn't do that" I look around and see Joe walking towards me "where am I?" He smirks and hands me a bottle of water "no more questions" he walks back towards the way he came and I shake my head "wait!" He turns around and sighs "what?" I look around and shake my head "why are you doing this? Why me?" He walks towards me and strokes my hair "because you are the only thing Brody cares about that will truly destroy him" I move my head away and shake my head "your wrong" he shrugs and turns around "we will see" I shake my head and pull the chains "let me go!" He disappears into the darkness and I look towards the water and spot a light on the floor, I reach down and see a clock with a timer of 3 hours "oh no!" I pull the chains and look around "help?!" I look at the clock again and pick it up and see a wire connected to it so I follow the wire towards the way Joe walked in from and see another clock "I got to get out of here." I reach into my pocket and pull my phone out "no signal. Typical!" I walk around as far as the chain will let me holding the phone up and smile when I get one bar "perfect." I press onto Brody's name and send him a message of my location and watch it send "yes!" I smirk and look around before sticking my phone back into my pocket and walking towards the chair and sit down "please get my message Brody" I take a deep breath and sit back and wait. I look back towards the clock and see 2 hours and 30 minutes "I got to do something to pass the time." I look around and hear footsteps "I can think of a few things that can help" I see Noah walk in holding paper and pens "what's that?" He hands me it and smiles "the boss wants to know everything you know" I look around and shrug "and the boss couldn't come ask me himself?" He rolls his eyes and sits down "just write." I smirk and start writing a few lines and hand him it "The Earth is round? Flamingos are born white?" He looks at me and shakes his head "what is this?" I shrug and lean back on the chair "you wanted to know what I know?" He rolls his eyes and flings the paper back towards me "about us and the James family" I nod firmly and laugh softly "you should have said." I place the pen on the paper and take a deep breath "I can't write" I look at Noah and smirk "why not?" He looks at me and raises his eyebrow "my pen broke" I smirk before snapping the pen in half and fling it on the floor "fine play that way!" He grabs the pen from the floor and storms of. I look at the clock and take a deep breath "2 hours" I look around and nod "I can still get out." I look at the bottle of water on the floor and pick it up before takin a sip 'wonder if this will work?' I look around before sticking the water over my wrist where the chains are and try free my hands. After a few attempts I feel my hands squeeze through the chains and I get free "yes!" I laugh softly and shake my head and start running down the opposite end of the cave. I see light so I run a little faster and hear my phone beep so I stop and quickly pull it out and see a text from Brody 'On my way' I shake my head and look around 'no Brody!' I text him but my phone battery dies as I send the text "dammit Brody." I run back inside and spot Joe looking around before running back the other way "shit!" I run towards the chair and sit down and hold the chains in my hands and look towards the way Joe went out and smile as I see him walking back in with Noah. "Hi" Joe looks at me and shakes his head "but you wasn't there a minute ago?" I raise my eyebrow and laugh sarcastically "I have been here the full time?" Noah rolls his eyes and shakes his head "she can't move Joe." A loud bang comes from the way they came in and Joe and Noah quickly turn around "go check it out and I will stay with her!" Joe nods before running of and Noah walks towards me and I smirk and lean back onto my chair "what have you done?" I shrug and laugh softly "nothing?" He looks towards the way Joe walked and I see Joe running towards us "it's them!" Noah looks at me and shakes his head "how did he find us?" I stand up and drop the chains and smirk "I told him." Noah looks at Joe and shakes his head "you didn't take her phone? Idiot!" He walks towards me and grabs my phone and breaks it with one hand and flings with broken pieces onto the floor "move!" He grabs me and walks towards a large rock and pushes it and it opens "what will I do about them?" Joe looks at Noah and he looks at me and smirks "kill them" he looks back towards Joe and shrugs "all of them" The rock moves and it goes all black. "Move!" I feel Noah's hand wrap around my arm as he pulls me down "where? I can't see!" He laughs softly still continuing to pull me behind me "just follow me and don't try anything." After a few minutes I spot a torch ahead and Noah lets me go "just follow the flame" I follow behind him towards it and I see a room with CCTV screens and a sofa "what is this?" He walks towards the screens and grabs the remote "sit and no more questions." I sit down and watch the screens and eventually spot Brody on screen 2 running through the cave and when he reaches screen 8 Noah shakes his head and grabs a walkie talkie and presses the button "he's by the door!" I look at him and see him looking around before looking towards the camera "let the show begin." Noah smirks at me and looks back towards the screens and I watch and spot Joe and Deano walk out onto screen 6 and watch as they both try fight Brody "stop!" I stand up and Noah looks at me and smirks "enjoy the show" he walks towards me and smirks "I want to see it first-hand" I stick my hand into a fist and swing it towards his face hitting him as hard as I can. "You are going to regret that" he smirks at me and wipes blood from his nose "and I am going to enjoy this more now" he pushes me down and presses a button on the wall and a chain comes out the sofa and wraps around my arm not allowing me to move. "Enjoy" Noah walks towards the way we walked in and I shake my head and look at the screen "HELP!" I see Brody look around before looking at the rock we came in "Amy?!" I look at the screen and smile "Noah is!" Noah runs towards me and places his hand over my mouth before reaching for his walkie talkie "how can he hear her? I thought the room was soundproof?" He looks at the screen and the walkie talkie makes a noise "it is. He must be stronger than we thought" he looks at the screen and shakes his head "not another word from you." He looks around and takes a deep breath before tearing his sleeve and wrapping it around my mouth and walking away. I shake my head and pull my arm trying to get it free and after a few attempts I manage to get the sleeve away from my mouth and look towards the screen and see the rock move and Noah walk out and nodding towards Joe and Deano and they run of. Brody looks towards the camera and nods and has a conversation with Noah for a few minutes before Noah looks at the camera and sticks his thumbs up smirking "Brody!" Brody looks towards the rock and shakes his head before running towards Noah and they start fighting. I try free myself and look around the sofa and spot a black reset button so I press it and the chain goes loose and eventually falls onto the floor "yes!" I run towards the TV screens and spot a map of the caves so I look towards the TV Screens and see Noah lying on the floor and the secret door fall into a million pieces as Brody punches it. I smirk and run towards it and see Brody smile at me before falling to the ground "Brody?" I run towards him and bend down beside him "what happened?" He looks around and shakes his head "there was Viridi dust in the rock" I shake my head and bend down placing his arm around my neck "come on there is a way out down here." I walk down towards the other end of the cave with Brody's arm around my shoulder "come on, let's get you out of here." I carry him towards the exit and when I see the light I nod "you ok?" He smiles and tries to stand himself but falls onto the ground "come on we don't have much longer to go" he takes a deep breath and wraps his arm back around my shoulder as I continue towards the light. After a few more minutes I see the light get darker "what?" I look around and hear a girl laughing "Abbie!" I look at Brody and shake my head "what?" I look around and spot Abbie walk out from the shadows and smirk "hello Brody!" She looks at her nails and pulls out a bottle and smiles "nothing personal!" She flings the bottle and I see green dust inside so I fling my body onto Brody's and we fall over a Clift "hold on!"

Brody grabs me and holds onto the ledge "I got you" he looks at me and smiles "that looks heavy." His smile disappears and he shakes his head "no Amy!" I smile and nod with tears running down my face "it's ok." He holds onto my tighter and shakes his head "but I love you" I smile and take a deep breath before pushing my feet against the Clift wall freeing my hand from Brody's and fall into the darkness below. As I fall I close my eyes and smile "I love you too" I take a deep breath before blanking out unconscious. Brody manages to pull himself up with rage, he looks at Abbie and shakes his head "you will pay for that!" He runs towards her and pushes her against the rock "you wouldn't really hit a woman would you?" He smirks and shakes his head "hit you?" He looks her up and down and shrugs "I'm going to kill you!" He goes into his pocket and pulls out a small blue liquid and forces it down her throat and let's go of her, she falls to the ground and her body instantly turns burn and goes stiff "that was for Amy!" He wipes away a tear running down his face and walks back towards the way we came "this will all be for

Amy!" He starts to run and spots Jeremy and Liam standing by the rock "hey!" Liam spots Brody and smiles "it's over" he looks around and shakes his head "where's Amy?" Brody takes a deep breath and looks towards the ground "I couldn't save her" Liam laughs nervously and shakes his head "your joking right?" Brody smiles softly and shakes his head "I wish I was." Liam looks towards the way Brody came from and runs towards it "I don't believe you!" He looks around and takes a deep breath "Amy?!" Brody looks at him and shakes his head "I'm sorry, I couldn't save her." Liam runs towards Brody and grabs his t-shirt and pins him against the wall "well you should have tried harder!" Jeremy pulls Liam of Brody and shakes his head "what happened?" Brody nods towards the cliff edge that we fell down and takes a deep breath "we both fell and I couldn't hold onto her." Liam laughs sarcastically "why not? Not like she was heavy?" Brody shakes his head at him and looks towards the cliff "I had green dust inside me." Jeremy walks towards the cliff edge and looks down "I want to see the body before I go back and tell my fiancé that we just killed the only family member and only person she cares about!" Brody sits down and shakes his head "I can't" Liam rolls his eyes and walks towards the cliff "I will come with you" Jeremy nods and Liam jumps down "we won't be long" he jumps down leaving Brody himself sitting at the edge. Liam and Jeremy reach the bottom and look around "see her?" Liam looks at Jeremy and shakes his head "no, you?" He shakes his head and continues to walk around "you go down and I will go up?" Liam nods and walks down the cave as Jeremy walks up. After a few feet Jeremy turns around and takes a deep breath "any luck?" Liam stops and shakes his head "no but she has got to be here, right?" They hear a loud bang and run towards each other "is she not here?" They spot Brody and take a deep breath "we can't see her so maybe she got out?" Brody looks up and shakes his head "impossible!" He looks at Jeremy and shakes his head "right?" Jeremy looks at and shrugs "I don't know" he takes a deep breath and smiles softly "but it does seem like the only explanation so maybe it is a possibility." Brody shakes his head and runs down the cave "Amy?!" Liam and Jeremy follow behind him down the cave. The reach the end of the cave and Liam spots stairs "this is the end" he looks at Brody and shrugs "so what do you want to do now?" Brody looks towards the stairs and smiles "Amy?!" He runs towards the stairs and spots something at the side of them "it's Amy!" Liam and Jeremy run after him and Brody bends down and picks up my unconscious blue body "she's alive."

Printed in Great Britain
by ˙Amazon